Jane Tara is the author of *The Happy Endings Book Club*, as well as three novels in the Shakespeare Sisters series: *Forecast*, *Trouble Brewing* and *Hamlet's Ghost*. She has over twenty children's books published in Korea, and runs a children's travel publishing company called Itchee Feet. She lives with her partner Dom and their four sons in Sydney. Jane can be contacted via her website: www.janetara.com.

Also by Jane Tara

Forecast: Shakespeare Sisters
Trouble Brewing: Shakespeare Sisters
Hamlet's Ghost: Shakespeare Sisters

The Happy Endings Book Club

Jane Tara

First published by Momentum in 2013
This edition published in 2015 by Momentum
Pan Macmillan Australia Pty Ltd
1 Market Street, Sydney 2000

A CIP record for this book is available at the National Library of Australia

The Happy Endings Book Club

EPUB format: 9781760080587
Mobi format: 9781760080594
POD format: 9781760300500

Cover design by Carrie Kabak
Edited by Elizabeth Cowell
Proofread by Dianne Blacklock

Macmillan Digital Australia: www.macmillandigital.com.au

To report a typographical error, please visit momentumbooks.com.au/contact/

Visit www.momentumbooks.com.au to read more about all our books and to buy books online. You will also find features, author interviews and news of any author events.

For Dominique ... who sees me.

A happy ending was imperative. I shouldn't have bothered to write otherwise.

—E.M. Forster

Prologue

Three weeks after Christmas

Paige flipped the open sign on her bookshop door to closed. Happy Endings was shut for the day, so let the festivities begin. Everyone was here. And early, which was unusual, but it was the book club's first meeting of the year, so everyone was excited to see each other.

Paige stared out her shop window. London, resplendent in Christmas decorations only a few weeks before, was now weighed down by the bleakness of winter. Normally, she'd find that depressing, but tonight she had other things on her mind. She straightened a few books on the shelf near the door and made her way back to the counter. She tidied a pile of bookmarks that were sitting next to the register, free for the taking, and closed down her computer. She could hear everyone else laughing and talking at one hundred miles an hour.

"Come on, Paige," called Michi in her Aussie accent. "Let's get on with it."

"I'll be with you in a minute." Paige unwrapped the tulips Tilda had given her. They were beautiful and for a moment

1

tears threatened to erupt again. Fortunately Tilda appeared by her side with a vase and shooed her away.

"You finish up here so we can start," Tilda said, and gave Paige's hand a quick squeeze.

Paige made her way around the shop, quickly tidying and finishing up for the day. She switched off the main lights, leaving some sidelights on, which filled the store with a warm glow. She loved her shop, with its wood floors and oak shelves crammed with books. In one corner there was an unusual collection of sofas and coffee tables all on top of a rug she'd picked up cheap in Turkey. The reading corner, she called it.

In the opposite corner her assistant, Clementine, was tidying the children's section, which was always in disarray by closing. With her cherry-red ponytail and rosy cheeks, Clementine looked barely older than a child herself.

"That looks good, Clem. Time to sign off," Paige said. "Can you grab the wineglasses?"

Paige looked across at her friends, lounging on couches and chairs. They'd spent the past year getting together, initially to discuss books, but life and love and a lot of laughter had quickly crept into those meetings. Before long, many of them were catching up for coffee or a movie outside of their book club gatherings. They'd just immediately gelled.

Book clubs were tricky. Strangers came together, and no matter how compatible they seemed, if they didn't like the same books—or at least respect what the other members liked—then the club would die a quick and often painful death. Put the wrong people together and books made them bitchy.

"I'm not judging you for it, but I don't read romance."

"You haven't read *In Search of Lost Time*?"

"Did you hear her pronunciation of Fyodor Mikhailovich Dostoyevsky?"

Paige found it very tedious indeed. Paige's last book club experience had turned sour when Norma, the woman who ran it, constantly vetoed everyone else's suggestions. The group read *Wuthering Heights*, *Tess of the d'Urbervilles* and *The Age of Innocence*. Finally, on the evening they got together to discuss *The Road*, Paige broached what everyone had been thinking.

"Can we have a happy ending?"

Norma looked at Paige as if she'd just farted. "What do you mean?"

"Norma, I enjoyed revisiting some of the books we've read. But I think everyone here agrees, we'd like a happy ending."

Everyone did agree, which angered Norma even further.

Norma pulled at the gloves she was wearing. Norma always wore gloves. "If you're finding these classics challenging ..."

Paige shocked everyone in the room when she rolled her eyes and said, "Are you saying *Pride and Prejudice*, *A Room with a View* and *To Kill a Mockingbird* aren't classics because the reader feels hopeful afterward?"

"Literary fiction, by its very nature, is rather dark."

"Says who?"

"Excuse me?" Norma was visibly seething.

"Who says that literary fiction needs to be depressing?"

Norma seemed lost for words. Paige felt sorry for her. She knew Norma struggled with depression. But in Paige's opinion she didn't do herself any favors with the way she spent her time, swallowing antidepressants and curling up with Sylvia Plath. Something funny or hopeful would do her good.

"Perhaps we just have different taste," Paige said kindly.

"And how would you describe your taste, Paige?"

"I prefer to focus on the positive."

"How Panglossian." Norma gave Paige a look that would wither steel. "Life is difficult. Books that end happily are misleading."

"I disagree." Paige was over it. She stood and straightened her skirt. "I'm working on having one in real life. But in the meantime … I'll have them in books."

Paige never went back to that book club, but the incident with Norma was what motivated her to follow through on her life-long dream of opening her own bookshop in Muswell Hill.

The Happy Endings Bookshop.

Well, that was what she was going to call it until her husband Tim put a stop to it.

"Christ, it sounds like a massage parlor."

"It's a great name for a bookstore."

"Yeah, an adult bookstore with a little room out the back providing extra services," he said. "I was wondering how you'd make this little business of yours work. Promote happy endings and they'll be lining up down the street."

Turned out he'd know. But at that stage she was still taking his advice and decided to name the shop Paige's Pages instead. She went ahead and had the signs and website made. Then, two weeks before she was due to open, she discovered her husband was having an affair. It was her fiftieth birthday. His timing always had been dreadful. She packed her bags and moved out that night. The next day, she ordered new signs and renamed her shop Happy Endings. The shop was going to be her happy ending, or a least a part of it.

It was also what she promoted. Yes, she sold books of other genres, just as she read books of other genres, but her specialty was romance, and any story that had a happy ending. She knew that was an ambiguous category. A happy ending for one person might not be so happy for another. Or it might not be a happy ending, but a beginning, or even both, because they're often the same thing.

Paige was too old and had been hurt too badly to ever think again that a happy ending meant meeting someone and riding off into the sunset. As much as she enjoyed her romance novels, she knew that was unrealistic. Waking up one day and knowing you were okay and able to live life alone—that was a happy ending. It was certainly hers.

Paige's shop stocked an interesting and upbeat mix of titles. She regularly held author signings and talks, always with a positive theme. It was why, in a time when little independent bookstores were a dying breed, Happy Endings was doing okay. It filled a need.

A year ago Paige had decided to form the book club she'd always wanted to belong to: the Happy Endings Book Club. She asked a few of her regular customers to join, starting with Eva, who seemed lost, and Sadie, who came across as sexy and funny yet often hung around the store as though she needed someone to talk to. Paige's assistant Clementine brought her roommate Michi along. She also invited a couple of the local shopkeepers she'd become friendly with, like Tilda, who ran the florist up the road, and Amanda from the lovely little boutique opposite. Muswell Hill had a real community feel to it.

Everyone got together at their first meeting and agreed the club should have the same name and purpose as Paige's shop. And yes, there had been many jokes about that name over wine on that first evening:

"Who said going to bed with a book wasn't satisfying?"

"Get some real action under the covers."

"The fictional boyfriend always has a spine."

"The romantic hero: pick him up when it suits you."

"With a well written book, there's no premature ending."

The women had spent the first book club meeting laughing hysterically, which immediately secured their friendship. They all had a similar sense of humor, but they all got it, too. They all wanted it. They all yearned for their own happy endings, both in real life and in the pages of the books they read. But mostly, there was just that added magic that some groups have when they meet.

As Paige finished tidying the shelves, she couldn't help but smile. *Magic.* She saw it in a million different ways now.

"C'mon, Paige. Come tell us how you're holding up."

Paige made her way over to the group. She needed this tonight. She needed the support of these women. She needed to share her sadness and joy. She hadn't seen some of them since before Christmas. And while a couple of the women had been particularly supportive of her over the past couple of weeks, no one knew the whole story. She certainly did have a story to tell. She just wasn't sure they'd believe it.

Eva handed her a wine. "The floor is yours, my friend."

Paige

The universe is full of magical things patiently waiting for our wits to grow sharper.

Eden Phillpotts

One week before Christmas

Paige stared at the bottle of blood-red nail polish on the table in front of her and then turned back to her elderly mother.

"You want your toenails painted?"

"That's what I said."

"Now?"

"No, next week, when I might be dead." Jean propped a bare foot on her daughter's knee. Her toes looked as surprised to see the light of day as Paige was to see them.

Paige finally picked the bottle up. "Did you buy this?"

"One of the nurses bought it. I gave her the money."

"You don't think this color is a bit ... bold?"

"That's exactly why I chose it." Jean gave her daughter a wink, which almost knocked Paige from her seat. "I haven't always been this dull, you know."

Paige found that hard to believe. She'd often looked at her mother and thought, like many people did, that Jean would be beautiful, if only she put some effort into it. But it wasn't Jean Macintyre's style. She was the type of woman who bowed her head and walked faster if a man dared whistle her way. She wore high-buttoned blouses and sang loudly in the church choir. She never wore make-up, never painted her toes, and her hair, while neat and clean, was always cut efficiently short.

So who was this woman who suddenly wanted a pedicure?

"How's your hip today, Mum?"

"Good as new."

"Well, technically it is new. That's what a hip replacement is."

"They're telling me I could be back home by Christmas."

"That's only a week, Mum. We don't want to rush things." Paige didn't add that she also wanted her mother well enough to go back to her own apartment. She didn't think she'd cope living with her. "I think I should speak to your doctor."

"I told you, that's not going to happen. I'm not a child."

"I just think they should investigate what caused the fall, Mum."

"I told you, it was a little turn."

"And that's the proper medical term for it? A turn?"

"That's right." Jean stared at her daughter. "You should do your own nails after you've finished with me. You haven't made an effort for quite a while."

Paige ignored her mother and shook the nail polish. It was true. She hadn't made an effort now for more than two years. She'd given up the day she left Tim. She'd tried to stay attractive for her husband, and in the end it didn't matter. He left for a younger version of her anyway. And all Paige could think was why did she bother?

"Which foot do you want me to do first, Mum?"

Jean wiggled the toes on her left foot and Paige started painting. They sat in silence for a long time. Usually Jean chatted nonstop. Not about anything personal or important, but about the weather, local news. It was the type of conversation you had briefly with a neighbor, not over a period of hours with your only child. Paige always left with a headache. But today Jean was quiet.

"Something wrong, Mum?" Paige asked as she painted Jean's big toenail.

"No."

"Are you feeling unwell?"

"No."

Paige put her mother's foot down and lifted the next one. "You're awfully quiet today," she said as she shook the polish again.

"I'm thinking about your father."

Paige looked at her mother in shock. She *never*, *ever* mentioned Paige's father. Paige had been told he'd died when she was very young, that he'd been a perfectly nice man, but that it was best not to dwell on it. The few times Paige had tried to broach the subject of her father, she'd been firmly rebuffed. She'd learned early on not to speak of him.

"What about my father?" Paige spoke quietly. She didn't want to scare her mother into silence, for she knew this was a rare opportunity to glean some information about him.

"He was a dreadful shit."

Paige was so shocked she dropped her mother's foot. Jean didn't seem to notice and carried on talking.

"Couldn't keep it zipped. Had such a wandering eye. Probably still does."

Paige felt sick to the stomach. "Still?"

"The most magnetic man to ever walk god's earth. And handsome!"

Paige could feel her heart pounding. Handsome? She'd never seen a photo. What did her mother mean by *still*? Could she ... could her mother ... be losing her marbles? Was Alzheimer's setting in?

Jean smiled. "We met in Cornwall, where he lives ... It was quite unexpected. And love at first sight, for both of us. Ridiculous ... I knew from the beginning that it was an impossible match. But lord how I loved him."

Paige was gobsmacked. Was her uptight mother speaking this way about love? About her father?

Jean turned to her daughter and looked her square in the eye. "I don't think I'm long for this world, Paige, so I was thinking ... perhaps you should look him up."

"B ... but my father is dead."

"No, I lied. He's alive and well, and given who he is, he'll probably outlive you."

"What do you mean? Who is he?"

"Paige, dear, don't be shocked, but your father is a fairy."

*

Paige stumbled out of her mother's room and made her way to the empty visitors lounge nearby. Had her mother just told her that her father was gay? Is that why they split up? Is that why she never mentioned him?

She stared around the room, as if the answers would be there, in the generic framed landscape that decorated the white wall, or in the corner with the cheap Christmas tree covered in candy canes.

She put some money in the vending machine and bought herself a Coke, then sipped it while she tried to make sense of what her mother had just told her. Perhaps the strangest thing of all was the cheery, matter-of-fact manner in which she'd told her.

Paige shook her head. Impossible. Her father was not gay and he definitely wasn't still alive. She would have known. No one could keep such a secret without giving something away at least once. Certainly not Jean Macintyre, who found it difficult to keep secret what she'd bought someone for Christmas.

"I've just bought you a lovely nightgown, Paige. I know I shouldn't ruin the surprise, but I'm so excited. It was sixty percent off."

"Hi, Paige. Penny for your thoughts."

Paige looked up into the impossibly handsome face of Jean's physiotherapist, Arley Douglas, and immediately blushed, as she always did when she saw him. She was certain he noticed, but she comforted herself with the fact that Arley Douglas probably had this effect on most women, so he'd be used to it.

"Oh, hello, Arley, I was just ..." Paige let her words drift off and tossed the Coke can into the trash. "Pondering ... I guess."

"Is there a problem with your mother?"

"We can discuss it later. I know you're busy."

Arley sat on one of the lounges nearby. He stretched his legs out in front of him and cocked his head to one side as he searched her face. "No time like the present."

Paige had the urge to throw herself into his lap. Arley Douglas was the sexiest man she'd ever set eyes on. He had black hair, peppered gray at the edges, and blue eyes that crinkled slightly when he smiled, which was often. Every time she ran into him, she'd look into those eyes and strange feelings and memories would stir but not quite surface. He seemed familiar, and yet he was like no one she'd ever met. He was larger than life, and when he turned his focus on you, you felt like the only person in the world. He seemed to care. And as much as Paige reminded herself that he treated everyone the same way, it was truly nice to be in his company, even occasionally, because Paige was rarely around a man who seemed to care.

"I'm worried that my mother might have ... ah ... dementia or something."

Arley looked concerned. "What makes you say that?"

Paige fingered the locket around her neck. "Well, to cut a long story short—"

"Why?"

"Why what?"

"Why cut a long story short?"

Paige was thrown. "I don't want to bore you."

"Why would you bore me?"

"I ... just might."

"Because you think I find you dull? Or do you think I have a short attention span?" Arley pretended to be offended.

"No ... I mean ... I don't know you very well, but I presume your attention span is perfectly fine." *Why did he always turn her into an inarticulate fool?*

"So why do you think the long story would bore me?" Arley grinned at Paige. "I'd prefer the long story."

Paige stared at him in surprise. He was a most unusual man. Her ex, Tim, used to get extremely impatient with her if her stories went on for more than a minute.

"Okay, the long story it is ..."

For the next forty minutes, Paige found herself telling Arley things she'd never discussed with anyone, certainly not Tim. She told Arley about her childhood, her mother, how she felt about never meeting her father, how in many ways she chose Tim because at first his controlling ways seemed quite fatherly. And then, finally, she recounted the conversation she'd just had with her mother. She left out the bit about her father being a fairy, without quite knowing why, but she told him everything else.

"And so," she finished, "I can only conclude that she must be losing her mind … to suggest that my father is still alive … and would in all likelihood outlive me."

Arley nodded, as he'd done countless times since her tale began. "She may be a bit confused after the anesthetic, but that doesn't imply something as sinister as dementia. I work with a lot of dementia patients and I've certainly never seen any warning signs with your mum. She's as sharp as a tack." He paused for a moment, and then added, "And a dreadful flirt."

Paige blinked a couple of times. Had he mixed his patients up?

"My mother is Jean Macintyre in room 76. With the hip replacement."

Arley's eyes twinkled. "Even if I'd forgotten your mother, Paige, I'm certain I wouldn't forget you."

Paige felt her cheeks flush again. Damn them! "It's just when you say she's a flirt … that's not normal behavior for her."

"Is that so? She seems awfully good at it."

"Do you think it's tied in with what she said to me?"

Arley didn't seem to be concerned. "It's not like she said anything completely outrageous."

"There was one more thing she said that's rather … outrageous. One thing I haven't yet told you." Paige was embarrassed now. "She told me that my father is … gay."

"Gay?"

"A homosexual."

Arley's eyebrows shot up. "She said he's a homosexual?"

"Well, no, the exact word she used was *fairy*, which is so typical of her narrow-mindedness, to even use that word. She said, Paige, your father is a fairy and lives in Cornwall."

Arley stared intently at Paige for what seemed like an eternity, his sea blue eyes searching deep into her own. Finally he said, "Why don't you go back in and ask her more about it?

The very fact that she's even mentioned it, after all this time, means she wants to talk." Arley stood and smiled reassuringly. "Then, afterward, drop by and see me. And if you're still concerned, I'll talk to her doctor."

"I appreciate that. She won't let me speak to her doctor."

"Fair enough. She's elderly, but wants to remain independent."

"Well, that won't happen if she has dementia, will it?"

"Go and talk to her, Paige. Ask questions. And be open to what she says.'

Paige nodded. Arley was right. She needed to find out as much as possible while her mother was in the mood to talk. "Thanks for listening."

"No, thank you for sharing." And with that he sauntered out in such a sexy way that it was impossible for Paige to not check out his butt. For a moment she almost felt young again. Then she remembered her own butt and the feeling passed.

*

Paige returned to her mother's room to find Jean flicking through a copy of *Vogue*.

"I thought you'd left."

"I was talking to Arley."

Jean's face lit up. "He's a sexy man."

Good lord, was this her mother or an impostor planted by aliens?

"He's about your age too," Jean added. "And single ... so I'm told."

"By who?"

"By him, when I asked him."

Paige shook her head. How had her buttoned-up mother ever become relaxed enough to ask her physiotherapist such a question?

"I think you two have an awful lot in common. Perhaps more than you realize."

"Well, unless he spends most nights alone eating Marks & Spencer dinners while flicking through book release catalogues, that's unlikely."

"You could ask him out," Jean suggested.

"Pigs will fly first."

"There are stranger things out there than flying pigs, dear."

Paige decided to ignore her mother and take control of the conversation. "I need to know, Mum, what makes you think my father was—?"

"A fairy?"

"Well, yes, I guess ... for want of a better term. I'm not sure that's appropriate, but yes."

"He told me," Jean said

"He told you?"

"Yes. I didn't believe him at first. As you can imagine, I was shocked. But then he introduced me to all the other fairies. I went to some fairy parties with him. I had fun ... everyone so happy and gay."

Paige yanked at her collar. The room was so stuffy. "So how long before you left him?"

"Two years. Around the time you were born."

Paige looked at her mother in horror. "You stayed with him, and fell pregnant, despite what you knew about him?"

"I know, but I was in love. The reality only hit home when I became pregnant. I knew having a little half-blood—"

"Half what?"

"Well, you're half his, Paige, whether you like it or not."

"Yes, but that doesn't make me half gay ... or bisexual ... or anything."

"What on earth are you talking about?" Jean was completely baffled.

"Having a gay father doesn't make me half homosexual."

"Who said your father was a homosexual?"

"You did."

Jean looked at her daughter as though she was nuts. "I did not."

Paige began to panic. Her mother really was losing her marbles. "You did. All afternoon you've been saying that my father was a fairy."

Jean shook her head at her daughter's stupidity. "Honestly, Paige, you've never listened to me, have you? I didn't say your father was gay. I said he was a fairy. One of the little people that live under the hills in Cornwall."

*

Paige's hand shook as she knocked on Arley's door. How cruel old age could be. Her mother had always been the most sensible woman she'd ever met. For her to be reduced to this babbling, delusional creature was almost more than Paige could bear.

"Come in," Arley called.

Paige entered the room and he waved her into a chair.

"So how did it go?"

"Not as well as I ..." And with that Paige burst into tears. "Oh, I'm so sorry. I feel like I've been such a bother all day. But I'm dreadfully worried about her. She's completely lost her mind."

Arley pushed a box of tissues toward Paige and waited patiently for her to stop crying. Then, once her eyes were dry, he continued.

"What makes you think she's lost her mind?"

"When she told me my father was—is—a fairy, she didn't mean gay. She meant ..." Paige's eyes opened wide. "She believes he's a fairy."

Arley nodded. "Yes."

"A fairy," Paige said again.

"Right."

"A *fairy*. As in pixies, goblins and fairies."

"Three completely different races, but yes, I understand what you mean."

Paige was bewildered. Arley either didn't understand at all, or he didn't think it was that shocking. "I think my mother has dementia," she said.

"There's only one way to find out," he told her.

Paige nodded. A meeting with the doctor. A round of tests, no doubt.

Arley's eyes twinkled. "You'll have to find out if your father is alive."

*

Paige spotted Eva at their regular table in the far corner of the small Indian restaurant. She still did a slight double-take when she saw her friend. Eva had only recently decided to stop dying her hair and embrace the gray. She now had a silver pixie cut that, if anything, made her even more beautiful. She was one of those knockout women at any age, with curves in all the right place, incredible eyes and cheekbones to die for.

Eva saw her and gave a wave. Here they both were well past middle age, yet Paige often felt like they were two kids, always so thrilled to see each other. She needed to see Eva tonight. She was so wound up about her mother.

Jean had been a devoted parent, but not a warm one. She'd always kept Paige at arm's length. There were times Paige would catch Jean watching her and she'd have the strange feeling that the look in her eyes was one of regret. Their relationship was built on habit and responsibility rather than affection, but even so, she was filled with fear at the thought of her mum disappearing into the abyss of dementia. As frustrating as Jean could be, she was the only mother Paige had, and it was a comfort to know she was there.

Paige gave Eva a kiss and relaxed as she took off her coat. It was cold outside, but nice and warm in here.

Paige glanced at the menu. "Have you ordered for us?"

Eva nodded. "All sorted. Masala mushroom, aloo jeera and some samosas for starters. Now tell me about your mum."

Paige gave her an update. She gave her all the details, including the bit about her father being a fairy and living in the hills of Cornwall. Eva nodded and asked a few questions, and a couple of times reached across the table and patted Paige's hand.

"So have you spoken to Jean's doctor?" Eva asked.

"No, Mum doesn't want me to. She said children should only take over dealing with their parents' doctors when those parents are in adult nappies."

"She's got a point. So what did this sexy physiotherapist say?"

"Did I say he was sexy?"

Eva laughed. "No, but I could tell you think it by the way you blushed when you said his name."

Paige rolled her eyes. "I'm so pathetic."

"Au contraire, my friend. It's a charming quality, and I'm sure the physio agrees."

"Well, it doesn't matter how sexy he is, I think he's as mad as my mother."

"Why do you say that?"

"Because his solution is for me to go and find my father." She gave her friend a look that said, *Can you believe it?*

"Your real father who's been dead for years, or the fake fairy one?"

"Arley says it won't do any harm, and will show my mother that I'm supportive of her."

"He has a point. I had an uncle with dementia and it's incredibly hard to diagnose. They deteriorate so gradually, over time. And the early stage dementia patient can feel frightened by their lack of recall."

"So you think I should follow his advice and go hunting for fairies?"

"Darling, what harm will it do?" Eva said.

"I have a bookshop to run."

"I'm sure fairy hunting can take place outside of trading hours."

Paige was quite surprised by her friend. "You don't believe all that supernatural stuff, do you?"

Eva stared at the wall behind Paige for a moment. "I don't know. Sometimes I have this overwhelming sense that Geoff is with me. Once or twice I've caught something in the corner of my eye, but when I've turned my head, nothing was there."

Paige gave Eva's hand a squeeze. They'd met not long after Eva's husband had died, when Eva joined Paige's book club, and had become fast friends.

"What surprises me each time is ... how dreadfully disappointed I've been when I turn and nothing's there. Like deep down I do believe Geoff's spirit could drop by and comfort me. And here I was thinking I was a skeptic." Eva blinked away the tears and smiled. "I don't know what I believe anymore ... but the world is a much nicer place with the possibility of magic. Don't you think?"

"I've never thought about it. I just think what you see is what you get," Paige said.

Eva nodded thoughtfully. "And I think that's our problem."

*

"Paige!"

Paige turned around the see Arley striding down the hall toward her. Her hand instinctively shot up to check her hair.

"I've been thinking about your mother," Arley said.

I've been thinking about you, thought Paige, but nodded.

"Why don't you drop by after you've seen your mum? I have someone you should talk to."

"A specialist."

Arley gave her a mysterious smile. "Yeah, she's a specialist. In her field."

Paige nodded. "That would be great. Thank you."

Arley cocked his head to the side. "By the way, your hair looks lovely today."

Paige willed herself not to blush, and despised herself when she did. "Thank you. It's nice of you to notice."

She quickly turned and walked away toward her mother's room. She prayed he wasn't watching her. She felt almost certain that he was, but she'd rather eat bugs than turn around to see.

*

Paige was completely stunned to find her mother wearing lipstick. She couldn't ever remember her mother wearing lipstick before.

"Where did you get a lipstick?" Paige asked.

"One of the nurses bought it for me."

"I would've bought you some, Mum. All you had to do was ask."

"Don't take this the wrong way, dear, but do you even know what lipstick is?"

Paige felt miffed. She knew she didn't spend much time or money on make-up, but it wasn't as though she made no effort at all. "I wear mascara," she said, sounding slightly defensive.

"You do, and your eyes are all the better for it."

"Mum, we need to speak. About what you told me yesterday."

Jean glared at her daughter. "Fine … just don't use that tone with me."

"What tone?"

"The tone you're using now. People use that tone with toddlers and dementia patients. And usually for the same reasons. They don't want them throwing tantrums and soiling themselves."

Paige readjusted her tone. At least, she hoped she did. "Okay, Mum—I'm sorry. But what's this about my father being a fairy from Cornwall? It just doesn't make sense."

"Very few things in life do."

"Mother, fairies aren't real."

"They are."

"They aren't."

"Says who?"

"Says … I don't know, me and every other sane person."

Jean sighed. "You think I've gone mad. I can see it in your eyes. Alzheimer's fear. You don't want to look at me in case you fall into the same abyss."

"You seem sane, Mum, but surely you can see the changes."

"What changes?"

"The nail polish. The lipstick."

Jean propped herself as high as she could and held her chin in the air. "I was quite a looker once, you know."

"I'm not suggesting that you weren't. Or aren't."

"I was the most stunning woman in Cornwall. And I have no problems admitting that. A man like your father would never ever cross over for anything but the best."

Paige let her bulging eyes do the talking.

"After I left your father, I went into hiding. I don't kid myself. He could've found me. But I made sure he wouldn't want me. That man was like a drug … and the only way out was to go cold chicken."

"Turkey."

"What?"

"It's cold turkey. Not cold chicken."

"Whatever. To make the break, I made myself look ... fowl." Jean laughed at her own joke. "What's up, you didn't find that funny?"

"No, I didn't," snapped Paige. "I'm too busy trying to wrap my head around all this." She massaged her temple. "So why the sudden change? Why now?"

Jean's voice verged on hysterical. "Firstly, I'm sick of being a bloody frump. It's not me, and it's never been me. I miss dressing up. I miss it, I tell you."

Paige was completely taken aback by her mother's outburst. "Mum, I had no idea."

"I did it to protect you. I don't have to now. You're old enough to know. And I'm old enough to wear lipstick again. Because quite frankly ... even if your father walked through that door now, he wouldn't look twice at me. I'm too old."

Paige glanced over at the door. She couldn't help herself.

"Don't worry. He won't walk through it." Jean sounded disappointed.

"I wasn't expecting him to," Paige said, feeling foolish. For a moment she *had* almost expected a strange man to come striding in. Everything else was strange and crazy and upsetting. Who knew what would happen next?

"All these years, Mum, and you've never said a thing."

"It was never my intention to tell you. I figured I'd go to my grave with it."

"But then you decided to go to your grave wearing lipstick."

"It's more than that." Jean looked pensive. "I made a mistake. I should've told you, when you were young. It might've made a difference."

"To what, Mum? I don't understand."

22

Jean stared at her daughter and then blurted, "You're so much like me."

"Is that a bad thing?" Paige innately knew it wasn't a great thing.

"It's my fault. I stripped the world of all its magic, thinking I was protecting you. But now I'm not so sure. You're so …"

"So?"

"Solid."

"Solid?"

"A bit dull," said Jean. "You're smart, and you certainly did the right thing divorcing Tim. What an insipid excuse for a man he was. You need to fall madly in love. That's what you need."

Paige's mouth was open in disbelief. "You think I'm boring?"

Jean reached out and took her daughter's hand. "No. I think your view of the world is boring. There's so much more to it, but I stood in the way of you exploring that. I was trying to protect you from your father's world. But that might be the exact thing you need, Paige." Jean smiled sadly at her daughter. "Do you see what I mean?"

"No, I don't." Paige was confused.

Jean sighed. "Exactly."

*

Paige didn't stop by Arley's office after talking to her mother. She was too upset. And after all, he was her mother's physiotherapist, not her doctor or shrink. She shouldn't really be talking to him about anything that didn't involve her mother's hip or aged care rehabilitation. All these conversations about fairies! The guy must have thought she was mad.

She went straight home instead, to her flat above her bookshop. She felt like the world was out of kilter and her little flat was the one place she still felt safe.

Tim had originally bought the building as an investment. (Tim liked investing in property, just not in marriage.) The intention had been to open the bookstore and run it without rental overheads, and to lease out the flat above it. During the divorce, Tim had been an utter bastard. He wanted the house, and the investment properties in Hounslow and Lewisham, and the three in Spain. Paige had agreed, but only if he signed over this building, which he had. Grudgingly.

Some of her friends were amazed that she didn't demand more, but she didn't need more. She didn't want more. Paige renovated the apartment upstairs for herself. She had her shop and her apartment and she had her freedom.

The flat was small, but lovely, with large bay windows in the lounge that captured the sun. There were wood floors throughout, with high ceilings, and French doors opening to a small patio, where she grew herbs. There were two bedrooms and the bathroom had a claw-foot bath. She had plenty of cupboard space and, importantly, shelves for her books. She had central heating, a reasonably modern kitchen, and her own entrance. It was home, it was hers and she loved it. It was usually a very comforting space. Usually, but not tonight.

Paige tossed her keys and phone on an entrance shelf. She noticed a text from her daughter, Linda. "Just wondering if you've made a decision on spending Christmas here? I need to order the turkey." She'd reply tomorrow. Paige adored her daughter, but their relationship had been strained since she'd left Tim. Of all people, she'd expected her daughter to support her. But Linda, a professor of criminology at the University of Cambridge, had taken her mother's inability to forgive her father as a personal insult. She felt the divorce and the bookstore were Paige's midlife crisis, conveniently ignoring Tim's affair and much younger new wife.

I wonder how she'd feel about having a fairy grandfather? thought Paige.

Paige paced up and down, pausing to stare out the window at regular intervals. She tried to eat, but couldn't. She opened a bottle of wine and had a glass, but it didn't help. Eventually, she grabbed the keys to the shop and made her way downstairs, into the shared entrance, and opened the back door of the shop. She'd always thought it was like entering a fairyland at this time of year, with the shimmering, twinkling Christmas lights she'd installed. But this time, for just a moment, she wondered if that was what fairyland really looked like.

"Perhaps my father can tell me," she muttered as she switched on the main lights overhead.

She began to search the shelves and found a book on dementia. She scanned a few pages, but it wasn't her mother she was reading about. The symptoms weren't familiar. *Memory loss.* Jean seemed to be remembering things rather than forgetting them. She read down the whole checklist. There was nothing there that indicated her mother was in the early stages of dementia—but instead of bringing comfort to Paige, this realization filled her with terror.

If Jean didn't have dementia … then …

She placed the book carefully back on the shelves and walked around to the new age and spirituality section. There, she pulled out a couple of books she'd stocked on a whim: *A Real History of Britain's Fey Folk* by Rebecca Morris (an Oxford scholar) and *Cornish Folklore* by Wendy Newbury (a Cornwall-based psychic). Paige pulled up a small reading stool and perched herself on it, the books on her lap.

"I can't believe I'm even considering this … and I can't believe I'm talking to myself."

She opened the history book and read the first few pages. While interesting, it was rather dry and academic—not quite what she was after. She slid it back onto the shelf and opened the book on Cornish folklore. She read about giants and mermaids, knockers and piskies, and King Arthur. But while the book was beautifully illustrated, it was as helpful as the book on dementia.

Zap! The light flickered off. Paige had just enough time to tell herself that the bulb must've blown before it came back on. She shivered. She suddenly felt very cold, despite the heating. An icy breeze tickled the exposed skin on her neck. She knew it was just her imagination, but she felt frightened and wanted to get back upstairs.

As she put the book back in its place on the shelf, she noticed a small, battered little book beside it. She knew immediately that it hadn't been there earlier. She'd never seen it before and felt uneasy. She considered leaving it, and praying that tomorrow it would be gone. But curiosity got the better of her and she drew it out anyway.

The book was slightly larger than the palm of her hand and bound in worn brown leather. There was a small title on the front in gold lettering, but in an unfamiliar alphabet.

Paige tentatively opened the cover. There was no imprint page, or any way to tell when it had been published or who had published it. It appeared to be handmade. The pages seemed to be made of fine gold. She turned another page to discover a sketch of a woman in an unusual type of ink. The woman was breathtakingly beautiful and dressed in what appeared to be royal garb. On the next page was another drawing, of a man, equally attractive. The next page contained a drawing of them both together, holding a child. More pages, more drawings, more faces and people, each page becoming more and more fantastical with strange creatures and worlds.

Paige's body filled with an icy dread. Where had this book come from? And why did she feel like she was being watched?

She flipped the book over and on the back cover was one word in gold lettering: *Paige*.

*

Paige usually had more restraint but this morning she couldn't wait for a suitable time to visit. She was up. Hell, she hadn't slept. So why should her mother? She marched into her mother's room at 7:30 am, expecting to find Jean asleep. Instead, she was in the chair beside her bed. She was fully dressed, her hair had been styled, and she had a visitor. It was Arley, sitting in another chair he'd pulled up to face her. They were deep in conversation and he was holding her hand.

There was a moment of uncomfortable silence when Paige entered. "Am I interrupting something?"

Arley stood. "All good. I was just leaving." He gave Paige a warm smile as he left.

Paige breathed his scent in as he walked past her. God, he made her dizzy. She realized her mother was watching her with interest.

Paige stalled. "You're wearing lipstick at this time of the day?"

"I leave it on. I've decided I've wasted too many years looking like death, so when I actually do die, I want to be wearing Revlon Really Red."

"So you're sleeping in it?"

"One can never be too careful at my age. Every night some poor bugger dies around here. When it's my turn, I'm checking out with red lips."

"Don't be so melodramatic. This is a rehabilitation clinic, Mum, not a nursing home." Paige thrust the book at her mother. "What's this?"

Jean refused to take it, so Paige poked her with it a few times.

"Get that away from me," Jean squealed.

"What is it?"

"I don't know, but I sense that I don't want to touch it."

"You *sense* you don't want to touch it? What do you mean by that?"

Jean looked wary. "One must be very careful what one accepts, when it's from those bloody Fey folk."

Paige thrust it at her mother. "Take it!"

This time, Jean did as she was told. She held the book like it was the hand of a leper, and carefully opened it, landing on the page with the illustration of the man, woman and child. She stared at it for a moment, then slammed the book shut and thrust it back at Paige. "No idea. Never seen it before in my life."

"You're lying." Paige eyeballed her mother. "Don't you dare tell me my father is a bloody fairy and then clam up when things start to get even weirder. Where does this book come from?"

"I don't know. Where did *you* find it?

"In the shop, and I didn't put it there."

"They have a way of being everywhere. It's a sign. He's reaching out."

"How do you know?"

"Because that drawing is of us. Of him."

Paige closed her eyes for just a moment to regain her balance. "That's my father?"

Jean nodded. "Holding you. Me beside him."

"That's you?"

"I told you I was a looker," her mother said defiantly.

Paige studied the picture with great intensity. "My father?"

"Yes ... your father. Cadoc," Jean's tone softened slightly. "You have a father, and you should go find him. What's the worst that could happen?"

Paige looked her mother in the eye, something she hadn't done for a very long time. "The worst that could happen? I could find out you're right."

*

Paige marched straight over to Arley's office. Despite her resolve yesterday not to involve him in her problems, she wanted to see the specialist he'd told her about.

"Everything okay with your mother?"

"Yes, she seems fine, in her red lipstick. My world has been completely turned upside down though."

"What fun." Arley's blue eyes twinkled.

Paige looked at him as though he too must be mad. He might be the most magnetic man she'd ever met, but he also said some rather odd things. She knew it should put her off, but instead it stirred a pool of excitement in her gut. It was as though his presence offered the promise of adventure, and she was both excited and terrified by that.

"You mentioned there was someone I could talk to. A specialist."

"Yes. You'd like to see her?"

"Yes ... can you refer me?"

Arley gave her a nod. "Okay, you're referred."

"Excuse me?"

"I just referred you." Arley laughed. "You don't need a referral, Paige. You just need to show up. How about I take you and introduce you to her?"

"I'd appreciate that."

"Her work hours are a little odd. Why don't you meet me here at nine and we'll head on over."

Paige glanced at her watch. "Okay, that gives me just under an hour."

"No, I mean 9 pm."

"Tonight?" Paige was thrown. What the hell would she wear? Her next thought was that perhaps *she* was regressing, not her mother. She was acting like a teenager. It wasn't a date. As much as she'd like it to be.

She nodded in a way that she hoped indicated that she knew it was a professional meeting. "I'll see you back here at nine this evening."

"Great." Arley gave her a wink. "It's a date."

*

Paige knew it wasn't *really* a date, but she still wanted to look fabulous. She discarded one piece of clothing after another. Too dressy, not dressy enough, mutton dressed as lamb. Her wardrobe was a wasteland.

She grabbed her bag and keys and bolted out of the house. She couldn't do this alone. She needed advice, so she headed for the Pantry, across the road from her shop.

The Pantry was a gorgeous little boutique, owned by Amanda. Paige had watched Amanda come and go every day for a year before she'd finally introduced herself. Amanda was an immaculate brunette who was probably about forty but looked younger. She had class. She had style. Paige had found her intimidating until one afternoon when Amanda had come into Happy Endings and headed straight for the romance section. What Paige discovered that afternoon was that Amanda was also warm, and funny, and a little lonely after her divorce. Paige invited her to join the book club and friendship quickly followed.

Amanda's face lit up when Paige entered the store. "Hello, love."

They exchanged kisses and Paige plopped her bag on a chair. "I need your help. A whole outfit. Style me."

"Do you have a date?"

"No ... but I want to dress like it's one."

Amanda gave Paige a nod. Challenge on. She swept around the shop, pulling clothes off racks. Not lots. Just a few pieces that together formed one outfit. Then she handed everything to Paige and ushered her into the change room.

Amanda chatted to Paige through the dressing-room door. "What are you doing for Christmas?"

Paige slid a sweater over her head. "No idea. Linda has asked me to spend it with her and her husband, but I'm waiting to see if Mum will be allowed home. How about you?"

"I asked Peter and his new girlfriend over."

"No! Are you comfortable with that?"

"Christ, no. I totally regret it, but it was one of those moments where the kids were pushing for it, and I was put on the spot."

"Can you cancel?"

"I wish," Amanda said. "I'll probably just drink too much instead. That's what Christmas is for anyway, right?"

Five minutes later, Paige barely recognized herself.

Black wool pants and ankle boots, a gray and blue striped sweater and a well-cut dark gray tweed blazer. She knew it was a great outfit. It suited her, although she'd never have pulled it together herself. Thanks to Amanda, tonight she was going to embrace being fifty-something and fabulous.

"What do you think?" Amanda asked with the confidence of someone who already knew the answer to her question.

Paige beamed at her. "I think I'll take the lot."

A few hours later, Paige dug around her bathroom and found her make-up bag. It hadn't seen the light of day since she'd moved in. She applied some make-up, keeping it natural, but accentuating her eyes. She thought of her mother as she did, and smiled. Jean would be pleased.

Next she took a good long look at herself in the full-length mirror on the back of her bedroom door. She wasn't bad—still slim, though she had always been short—and her dark hair was glossy, although that now came from a bottle. Her skin was good, her eyes probably her best feature. She had been quite beautiful when she was younger, not that she'd

ever appreciated it, or taken advantage of it at the time. It's often only as beauty fades that it becomes apparent it was ever there, she thought ruefully.

But something sparkled back at her in the mirror tonight. It was her mother, or at least a glimmer of her. Not the version of Jean she'd grown up with, but the real Jean, the Jean who, if everything she said was true, had sacrificed herself to protect her daughter.

For years Paige had been petrified of turning into her mother. Now, for the first time in her life, she felt that wouldn't be a bad thing.

*

Paige was surprised to discover that this *specialist* worked out of a pub in Highgate. Alarm bells immediately rang, but she followed Arley into the King & Mistress anyway. The specialist could've worked in a Taliban training camp and Paige would've followed Arley there.

It was warm inside, and quite packed. A bluesy version of some traditional Christmas carols played in the background, and a Christmas tree shimmered in the corner. It was a quirky pub, welcoming and cozy. And Arley obviously knew the place well. He marched across the room and gave a woman behind the bar a friendly wave.

She blew him a kiss. "Arley, love, good to see you."

"You too, Batty."

Arley led Paige away from the main bar and through myriad smaller rooms. She felt like she should drop a trail of breadcrumbs to help find her way out. Then she looked at Arley's broad shoulders and firm ass and decided she'd rather follow those.

And so she did, through a corridor and down a set of stone steps into a small basement bar. A sign at the door said:

Calypso's Cauldron. Anyone who says alcohol never solves anything has never been here before.

Now Paige was starting to worry. Surely this was a professional visit and not a date. It was a bit late to ask him now. Instead, she looked around, to see if she could spot a dementia specialist, or at the very least a GP.

The room was lovely, with oak-lined walls and a stone floor. It had low ceilings and was dominated by a large, ornate bar. The lighting, while dim, was welcoming. There were candles and lanterns scattered everywhere and the glow from an open fireplace. Two long, rustic tables were surrounded by stools and by the fireplace were a couple of Empire armchairs paired with genuine Victorian footstools. Groups were seated at the tables and a few people milled together by the open fire. Others crowded around the bar, mesmerized by something hidden from Paige's view.

She followed Arley toward the front of the room and saw what everyone was looking at: the most stunning woman she'd ever laid eyes on. Flaming red hair, alabaster skin, green cat's eyes. Paige stood on her tiptoes and looked across Arley's shoulder. The woman was making a cocktail. Jesus! He'd brought her to a cocktail bar. This *was* a date.

As if he could read her thoughts, Arley turned to her. "Just in case you're wondering, this *is* work."

Just as disappointment flooded her face, he leaned forward and whispered in her ear.

"However, if it's a date you're after, I'm certainly available."

"Isn't that unprofessional?" Paige looked at him from under her lashes. She could almost feel the heat crackle between them.

"It would be if I asked your mother out. She's my client. Not you."

Paige surprised herself by saying, "I think I'll take you up on it."

For once, it was Arley who seemed embarrassed. Paige gave him a mischievous smile and turned her attention back to the redhead behind the bar.

The whole room stood still while the woman mixed. She grabbed a lemon, deftly sliced it in half and gave it a quick squeeze. Her hand slipped into a jar and returned with a pinch of something that filled the room with the smell of August rain. Her lips moved slightly, as if reciting an incantation, as she sprinkled it into the glass.

Paige watched her, transfixed. She was tall, with endless creamy limbs, her hair a tumble of burgundy waves. Paige glanced over at Arley, who seemed as dumbstruck as everyone else by the woman, and she suddenly felt a surge of jealousy.

God, to have him watch me like that!

Finally the redhead slid a cocktail across the bar toward a man, who tossed it quickly back. Paige looked around again. What on earth was going on? What was everyone waiting for?

After what seemed like an eternity, the man turned to the crowd with tears in his eyes. "It's gone. Totally gone. My fear of public speaking … even talking to you all now, it's not a problem." He threw his arms around a woman beside him, who looked equally thrilled.

The redhead clapped her hands. "See, and you were thinking of quitting your job over it. All it took was a little bit of fairy dust."

Paige felt sick. Was that why Arley had brought her here? To talk to this woman about fairies?

The redhead hadn't finished. She teased the man. "Before long your wife will probably bring you back in for a drink to shut you up."

"Never," laughed the man's wife.

People cheered and clapped and then returned to their own groups and conversations. Paige thought the whole scene was completely bizarre. She watched as the redhead surveyed the

room, until her eyes rested on Arley. Her face lit up and, if it were possible, became even more beautiful.

Paige noticed Arley motion toward her, and the woman's green eyes suddenly met her own. The woman watched Paige for a moment, motionless, and then, with a nod, she reached up to a bell over the bar and gave it a sharp clang.

"Closing time, folks. It's been grand, but please make your way upstairs."

Everyone did as they were told (Paige had a feeling this woman always got her own way), but Arley took Paige's arm and guided her up to the bar. He pulled out a stool for her and then opened the bar gate and stepped into the woman's embrace.

Paige had the sudden urge to stab the woman with a cocktail umbrella. How the hell could she compete with someone so young and stunning? Just as she was thinking of ways to make a graceful exit, the woman moved over to her, and embraced her too.

"Hello, Paige, I'm Calypso Shakespeare. It's always lovely to meet a friend of Arley's."

Paige felt quite tongue-tied, and for want of anything better to say, mumbled, "Your bar is nice."

"I'm glad you like it. Let me make you both a drink."

Calypso returned to her spot behind the bar and grabbed a cocktail shaker. Then she sliced an apple, grabbed a handful of frozen blueberries and a sliver of ginger and threw the whole lot in. Next in went a shot of rum and something else Paige didn't recognize—a blue liquid that seemed to glow. She gave it all a shake, and poured it into two highball glasses. Then, finishing it off, she placed a couple of cinnamon sticks in each glass and slid them across the bar.

"This is what you need."

Without thinking, Paige blurted out, "How do you know what I need?"

Calypso didn't seem the least bit offended. "Because it's my job."

Paige took the glass and sipped. Calypso was right. It was exactly what she needed. But the woman was still annoying.

"So Calypso, how's your dad?" Arley asked, breaking the tension.

"He's doing well. His tests have all been clear. He and Mum have a new lease on life. I can't tell you what a relief it is." She gave him a beatific smile.

Paige watched them chat over the rim of her glass. *Oh, get a bloody room!* She suddenly felt old and ugly in her new outfit. How could she compete with a woman who was clearly not wearing a bra?

"You've closed already?" a voice called from the door.

Paige watched as Calypso's eyes lit up. She turned and saw a man enter and suddenly felt like a fool. This man, this absolutely stunning man, was obviously Calypso's partner.

"Darling, look who's here," Calypso called.

The man strode across the room. "Arley. Good to see you."

The two men embraced and then Arley turned to Paige.

"Taran, this is a friend of mine, Paige."

Paige shook Taran's hand. She knew who he was—who didn't? She'd read all about Taran Dee, the artist from New York, but meeting him in real life packed a punch. He was tall, dark and beyond handsome. His face was perfect: chiseled, masculine, and yet beautiful. He had jet-black hair, a haughty nose and intense blue eyes. And from the way he looked at Calypso, Paige could tell he was a man in love.

She suddenly felt completely stupid. She had no right to be jealous. Arley and Calypso were just friends—and besides, Arley was only her mother's physiotherapist. She just wished she knew why he'd brought her here. Calypso asked the question for her, almost as if she'd read Paige's mind.

"So Arley, what's going on?"

Arley glanced at Paige, who wondered what he was going to say. Perhaps he was about to ask for a cocktail for early stages of dementia. Maybe Calypso didn't just make cocktails. For all Paige knew, she was a certified naturopath, or a neurosurgeon.

"Paige has just found out she's half Fey."

Paige almost fell off her stool. She waited for the laughter, but it didn't come. Instead, both Calypso and Taran nodded, as if they understood what a shock that would be for her.

Paige felt it best to explain herself. "My mother had a bit of a turn recently. She fell and broke her hip. Since then, she's been saying all sorts of things. I don't *think* she hit her head in the fall, but she might've."

Calypso smiled kindly at her. "You must have been frightened."

Her empathy threw Paige, who suddenly felt like crying. "It's certainly been a difficult few days."

Calypso looked deep into Paige's eyes. "I guess the question is … what if she's right?"

"She can't be."

"But what if?"

"Impossible," Paige said.

"Nothing's *impossible*," Calypso said simply. "What if your mother is right?"

Paige felt her chin tremble. "Then everything I've ever known and ever believed will be completely challenged."

Arley threw his hands up and looked ecstatic. "Isn't that great?"

Paige ignored him and instead focused on Calypso. "Are you saying you believe in fairies?"

"Yes. I work with them."

Paige glanced around the bar, half-expecting to see a drunken elf in the corner. "Here?"

"Usually in their realm."

Paige turned to the two men. "And you both believe in fairies?"

They answered in unison. "Yes."

Not a hint of doubt. They were both certain.

She turned on Arley. "How can you possibly believe in ... this?"

Arley took a moment before responding. "I have my reasons, Paige. I brought you here because Calypso not only believes in fairies but also has a good working relationship with the Fey folk around Cornwall."

"How convenient." Paige turned to Calypso. "I'm sorry, I don't mean to mock you. I just feel very confused at the moment."

And vulnerable, in this room of strangers.

Arley reached out and took her hand. It was a gesture that was meant to comfort her, and it did. She gratefully linked her fingers through his.

"So your father is Fey?" Calypso asked.

"That's what my mother says. She was madly in love with him."

"Fey men are certainly charming."

Calypso gave Arley a wink. A few minutes before it would've turned Paige green, but now it didn't bother her. It was her hand he was holding. And the heat from it was giving her strength.

"Do you have any more information about him?" Calypso asked.

"I came across an unusual book last night that ... and this will seem crazy ... appeared from nowhere."

The other three just nodded. They didn't seem to think she was crazy at all. She reluctantly withdrew her hand from Arley's, reached into her handbag and showed them the book. Calypso took it from her, her eyebrows raised as she searched through it. She paused at the drawing of Paige and her parents.

"That's my father, apparently."

Calypso turned the book around and showed Arley the image. Paige witnessed an unspoken conversation.

"Do you know him?" Paige asked.

Calypso nodded. "Everyone knows your father. This is Cadoc. King of Cornwall's royal Fey family.

*

"Lucky there's a doctor in the house."

The room swung back into view and Paige realized she was lying on the floor. Arley was leaning over her, a look of concern on his dangerously handsome face. Paige had the urge to reach up and kiss him, but then she remembered where she was … and that urge was replaced with the need to run.

"You're not a doctor, you're a physiotherapist."

Arley smiled. "Good, you remember who I am."

As if I could forget. "Did I faint?"

"I caught you," Arley said.

"How chivalrous." Paige sat up, annoyed with herself. "Just so you know, I'm not in the habit of fainting into the arms of men." She stared at him for a moment. "I haven't eaten much for a few days."

Arley helped her to her feet. "You're not the classic swooner type. You're in shock."

Calypso was on the phone. She replaced the receiver and started to fuss over Paige. "That was my sister. She's going to bring you something to eat from upstairs. My father runs a restaurant in the pub."

"Truly, I'm fine."

"How can you possibly be fine? You've just found out your father is Lord Cadoc."

"I don't even know what that means, Calypso."

"Not only that you're half Fey but that your father is the head of one of the most important royal households in all the Otherworlds."

Paige looked like she wanted to cry. "I'm just wrapping my head around the fact that I might have a dad."

"You need to catch up," Arley teased.

"Why do I get the sense that you're enjoying this?"

Arley reached out and brushed a lock of hair off her face. "Because I am."

"How does silverbeet with salmon rotolo, lemon cream and pine nuts sound?"

Paige didn't care how it sounded, because it smelled fantastic. She noticed her waitress looked a lot like Calypso, with the same color hair and porcelain skin. But this Shakespeare was much smaller, she wore glasses, and her hair was cropped short.

Paige recognized her. She was a customer from the bookstore.

The woman placed the dinner and a serviette on the bar and then tilted her head to one side. "I'm Nell. You own the bookshop down the road, don't you? I bought *Travels with My Aunt* from you last week." She handed Paige some silverware.

"That's right. I remember." Suddenly Paige was behind her bookshop counter again. "Did you enjoy it?"

"I loved it. I first read it years ago, but it was so nice to revisit." Nell touched Paige's arm, ever so lightly. "I hear you've had a big week."

"No doubt you believe in fairies too."

"Yes, I do," Nell said gently.

Arley nodded at the plate. "Eat, Paige."

She did as she was told, because the last thing she wanted to do was faint in front of everyone again.

While she ate, Nell looked at the book. She turned it over a few times in her small hands. "I've never seen anything like this before."

"Nell works for the British Museum," Arley explained.

Paige paused mid-mouthful.

"Not any more," Nell said, "I've just left and gone back to work for the British Museum of Romance."

Paige was doubly impressed. "I love that museum."

"Me too," Nell said. She ran her fingers over the gold lettering on the cover.

"What does it mean?" Calypso asked.

"I think it's a Fey language, perhaps even a local dialect." Nell placed the book back down on the bar. "That's all I've got for you. I've never seen anything like it before."

"What about the pages?" asked Arley. "What are they made of?"

"I don't know." Nell took a guess. "Fey gold?"

"It's a fairy photo album," Calypso chuckled.

"Maybe," Nell said. "Paige, I know someone who has studied Fey languages. Would you mind if I show it to him?"

Paige placed her cutlery on the plate and wiped her mouth with the linen napkin. Food was exactly what she'd needed. "I'd appreciate that, Nell. Thank you." Then she took a deep breath and looked at the others. "And in the meantime, how do I find my father?"

Clementine

*The hardest thing to see is what is in front
of your eyes.*

Goethe

One week before Christmas

From: SlamminSam@oinknet.com
To: ohmydarlingclementine@bokchoi.net
Subject: Happy anniversary

Hey baby! It's been three months since we cyber-met. I wish
I could say it's been three months since we first met face to
face, three months since I first kissed you. But we have to wait
a little longer for that. It will happen soon, I promise.

I know we were talking about me coming over for Xmas, but
I'm still unable to stand for long after the fall. The doctor said
the flight could do more damage to this back injury, and I want
it to heal. So be patient. As soon as I can fly, I'll be with you. The
wait will make our first meeting all the more amazing.

New York is totally wild at the moment. Christmas time is crazy. I wish you were here. I'd take you ice-skating at the Rockefeller Center, and walking through Central Park. (If my back was up to it.)

Let's have Christmas Skype sex.

Sam

*

From: ohmydarlingclementine@bokchoi.net
To: SlamminSam@oinknet.com
Subject: Re: Happy anniversary
Happy, happy, happy anniversary. Oh, I wish I was there with you. New York sounds so exciting. And I'd look after you while you're flat on your back. (Wink wink!)

It's cold and gray here in London, but I always do love Christmas. My parents are going to Spain again, but I said no this year, thinking you might be here. Not to worry. I'll probably spend Christmas with Debra and her aunt Tilda—although Debra has been a bit weird lately, so I'm not sure how enjoyable that will be. She might have girl issues. LOL. Who knows.

Michi has already gone back to Oz, so it's just me and Debra, who isn't speaking much. I'm feeling lonely. I wish you could come and cheer me up.

I hope you're not in pain.

Clementine

*

From: SlamminSam@oinknet.com
To: ohmydarlingclementine@bokchoi.net
Subject: Oh no!
I hate that you canceled your Christmas plans for me, and I let you down. I promise to make it up to you. Let's plan a visit

in the New Year. And I'll take you to Paris. The city of love, you, me … and ooh la la!

S x

*

From: ohmydarlingclementine@bokchoi.net
To: SlamminSam@oinknet.com
Subject: Re: Oh no!
Deal! Oh and can I have a postal address? Remember that book I was telling you about? Well, I ordered it in for you. I was going to give it to you for Christmas, but I'll express it over instead.

Michi

Christmas Day

Michi Downs was hot. Stinking, miserably hot. Christmas in Sydney had always been a bitch, but this was doubly bad, flying in straight from a London winter. Oh, how she missed the gray, cold, damp winter she'd left behind. Or at least that's what she was telling everyone, because any sign of weakness, any smidgen of homesickness, and her family would attack, and beat her into submission until she agreed to come home for good.

And that could never happen, because while she liked Sydney, it was also where her parents lived.

She watched them now from under her dark glasses and huge floppy hat. Her father Keith was manning the barbecue wearing one of those ridiculous aprons with boobs and a Santa hat. Her mother Kayoko was dressed in a sexy Santa outfit and carrying cocktails embellished with fruit and tiny umbrellas over to Aunt Yumi, who was lying topless by the pool. Michi was no prude, but Aunt Yumi (who for the record wasn't even related) was seventy-eight, so seeing her knockers out sunning themselves was enough to turn Michi off lunch.

Keith waved a piece of chicken around to get Michi's attention. "Will I throw a breast on the barbie for you, honey bunch?"

"No thanks, Dad. I'll stick to the salmon."

"It's beer o'clock," her younger brother said.

Michi looked up at Josh and gratefully accepted the beer he was holding. "I forgot how bloody hot it gets here," she said.

"You should visit more often." He threw himself into a chair beside her and kicked his long brown legs onto a nearby esky. "They miss us, you know." Josh took a swig of beer. "They might be weird, but they love us."

"Living overseas is … easier." She glanced at her brother. "How *is* Tokyo?"

"I'm not there to escape the family. I have dinner with Baba and Oji-chan twice a week."

Michi motioned to a couple seated at the outdoor dining set, looking somewhat ill at ease. "Have you met the Wagstaffs?"

Josh pulled his sunglasses off his head and down over his eyes. "There's no hope for them. Both have the sex appeal of a can of baked beans. Watching Kayoko and Keith go at it won't alter that."

"I can't believe they still let other people watch. At their age."

"Could be worse. A lot of people their age don't have any sex."

Michi rolled her eyes. She knew what that was like. "I just wish they'd keep it private."

Josh waved a hand around at the stunning Mosman home and large yard. "You too could have all this if you taught people how to fuck."

"I'll stick to my low-paying job, thanks." Michi nodded her head toward the Wagstaffs. "These ones at least have the decency to look ... nervous."

"They're carbon copies of all the others. Middle class, bored with their marriage but too afraid to leave it, and slightly starstruck by Mum and Dad."

"Do people still care?"

"Their royalty checks would suggest that they do."

Kayoko and Keith had been Australia's first real celebrity sex therapists. They were like your friendly suburban neighbors who just happened to have all the answers to a happy marriage. Kayoko came across as caring and ladylike, but she was also obviously a cracker in the bedroom if her columns in the *Woman's Monthly* were anything to go by.

Keith was like the bloke next door, only with a degree in psychology. When he'd started penning books and appearing on TV with Kayoko, their sex therapy brand became a national sensation. If Aussie blokes had to turn to someone about their sexual dysfunctions, then let it be Keith. Speaking to him, reading his books ... well, it was kind of like going fishing with a mate and admitting you were having problems with your rod.

Michi had grown up with this insanity. Whether it was via the admissions in their books or the inches dedicated to them in gossip columns, everyone knew all about Keith and Kayoko's sex life. Michi's friends at school knew. The local shopkeepers knew. Her lecturers at university knew. In fact, one of them had even seduced her, figuring it was the closest he'd get to his boyhood fantasy of banging Kayoko Downs. Michi didn't realize this until after he'd broken her heart. She'd been stupid enough to think he was interested in her, not her ageing mother.

She should've known better. Not many people had been interested in her, growing up, but her parents fascinated people. As a child she'd sit unnoticed under the dinner table while her parents and their assorted friends played footsies with each other. In fact, Michi and her brothers delighted in squeezing the hand or foot of unsuspecting bored housewives, which often prompted full-blown affairs. As a teenager she'd had to put up with naked pool parties thrown by her parents. She rebelled the only way she knew how. She was a straight A student and a virgin until she was twenty. Much to her mother's horror.

"You're holding onto it like the last Toblerone on earth." Her mother loved Toblerone.

"I'm choosy, that's all."

"It's just your virginity. It's more like a Cherry Ripe. Get rid of it." Another reference to chocolate, this time her mother's least favorite.

Michi's virginity had been such a traumatic topic that she still couldn't walk down the confectionery aisle in Coles without being haunted by it.

When she finally did lose her Cherry Ripe, Michi was disappointed. All that hype, and that was it? To be fair, her microbiology lecturer was not the ideal choice for her first lover. It was her final year of uni, and one afternoon after a particularly goading conversation with her mother, she'd allowed him to seduce her. He was apparently as let down by it as she was. He'd expected more, considering who her parents were.

The whole incident was so humiliating that Michi didn't even wait around for her graduation ceremony. She told her parents she was going to have a gap year in Europe, but secretly, she knew she was looking for a new life. Somewhere far away from her parents' notoriety. That was seven years ago.

"Merry Christmas, Michi-moooooo!"

Michi swung around at the sound of her old nickname. "Greg!" She leaped off her chair and gave her younger brother a huge hug. "I was wondering when you'd finally make an appearance."

Greg pulled his *I'm sorry* face. "I've been sooooo busy with work."

Michi put her hands on her hips. "Josh said you're on holidays."

"Okay, that's true. I've been soooo busy shagging. I met a fine-looking pharmacist a few days ago and I've been holed up with him, working on our own chemistry."

Michi noticed a man behind Greg: a drop-dead gorgeous man, with dark hair, muscular arms and an endless chest. He was more rugged than the men Greg usually went for. This was more like the type of man *she'd* go for. Not literally. She hadn't had a date in over a year. But if she were to, then Greg's new boyfriend was her type. She raised an eyebrow at her brother and stretched out her hand to the stranger.

"I'm Michiko, and I completely understand. I'm a huge fan of chemistry."

Greg burst out laughing. "Gawd, Michi, this is Jake ... I work with him. He's not the chemist. And he's straight." Greg threw Jake a wink. "Although I have tried to rectify that."

Jake laughed. "And it was tempting, mate, but I've chosen my team." He held Michi's hand longer than necessary.

Michi felt her cheeks flush. "Sorry, I thought ..."

Jake seemed amused. "All good."

Greg rolled his eyes. "I wish he was. Maybe next life."

Jake took it all in his stride. "So how's the homeland?"

Michi realized she'd been so flustered by his looks that she'd missed the accent. "You're English? Where from?"

"I grew up in Bristol, but I lived in London for years. Finsbury Park area."

"I'm in East Finchley."

"Home away from home," Jake said.

"Nope, just home."

Greg huffed, as he always did when he was bored by a conversation. "Here we go again ... *London's home ... Couldn't ever live in Australia now, oh no.*"

"It's not like that, Greg," Michi said defensively. "I'm just happy there."

"Whatever." Conversation over. Greg looked around the backyard. "Usual cast of suspects." His eyes paused on Aunt Yumi, and he screeched out, "Hey Yumes, have you had your tits done?"

Yumi lifted herself up onto her elbows, and it became immediately clear that she hadn't.

"No worries," yelled Greg. "False alarm."

"I've just perfected the art of lying," Yumi laughed.

"Me too," Greg said. "Remember that next time I compliment you on something."

Yumi thought he was hilarious. "You be careful, Greg, or I come over there and spank you."

"Make sure you don't trip on a tit on the way." He ripped off his shirt, displaying his gym-toned body. "I'm in for a dip. Anyone else?"

Greg dive-bombed into the pool, followed closely by Josh. Michi knew it was her turn next. Normally she loved going swimming with her brothers, but she'd rather stab toothpicks into her eye than let Jake see her in a bikini.

"You going in for a swim?" he asked.

"Maybe later." *After I've gone online and bought a burquini.* She sat and pulled a fresh beer out of the esky. "Want a drink?"

"Sure." Jake pulled up a chair beside her and cracked open his beer. He looked out over the view of the water. "This is a great place. I love all the bays and beaches around Sydney Harbour."

Michi gave the harbor a quick glance. "It's pretty, but Australia doesn't hold a candle to England's history."

Jake frowned. "Are you kidding me? We're sitting on land that has been inhabited for over forty thousand years."

"Good point. This was the Borogegal tribe's land well before Keith and Kayoko stuffed it up with their phallic-shaped swimming pool."

Jake turned and looked at the pool. "Yes, I was wondering if that was the design."

"It wasn't meant to be, but when they put the spa up that end and it looked like … er …"

"Testicles?"

"Yes, anyway, my parents were thrilled with the unexpected result. They celebrated by inviting *Outdoor Living Magazine* to do a piece on them. Charming photos of them skinny-dipping. Pure class, as always."

Jake watched her for a moment. It made Michi uncomfortable, as though it were she who'd revealed too much, not her parents.

"I like your parents," Jake said. "I spent Christmas Day here last year as well. They've been kind to me."

Michi looked at her dad, who was now regaling Dan Wagstaff with a tale about the art of withholding ejaculation. She glanced back at Jake, who was trying not to laugh.

"Admittedly, we're never had that conversation," he said.

The two of them burst out laughing.

Michi put her face into her hands. "Oh, take me back to London now."

Jake leaned forward and touched her knee. "No, don't go yet."

Alarm bells sounded in Michi's head. He was way too hot. He looked like the type of guy who got any woman he wanted, and was used to throwing flirtatious remarks around. She, on the other hand, found the whole flirting, dating, mating scene awkward. Most evenings she went to bed with a book, much to the amusement of her roommates, Clementine and Debra.

Michi turned away and concentrated on her warming beer.

Jake withdrew his hand. "So what do you do in London?"

Michi smiled. This would get rid of him. This was usually the cue for any hot guy to leave. "I'm an eye bank technician."

"Meaning?"

"I take tissue samples from dead bodies, and if they're suitable donors, I cut out their corneas."

To his credit, he didn't flinch. There was a moment's silence and then, with complete seriousness, Jake said, "*I see.*"

Michi groaned. "That's a *cornea* joke."

Jake broke out into a grin that made the hot Australian sun look dim. "Teach me about it. I'll be your *pupil.*"

Michi threw her head back and laughed. "That's a new one."

"Jokes aside, you must love it," Jake said. "It's not a job you'd do otherwise."

"I do love it," Michi said. "I took the job out of morbid fascination, but not long after I started working there, I ran into a woman at a party. It was a total coincidence. She'd had a cornea transplant and she told me all about the positive impact it'd had on her life. I went into work the next day knowing I was doing something worthwhile."

"How does one get into the field of harvesting eyeballs?"

"I did a biology degree, but one guy I work with got the job because he'd worked in a morgue and could lift dead weights."

Jake pulled a face. "Dead weights?"

Michi showed off a muscle in her arm. "I didn't get this from the gym."

"Has anyone ever told you you're a little Morticia Addams?"

"Oh, Gomez!" Michi mimicked. She glanced over at her brothers, who were seeing who could stay underwater longest. Nothing ever changed. "So you work with Greg?"

Jake nodded. "Yep. Been there about two years."

Michi looked embarrassed. "What does he do again?"

"Web design."

"That's right. So you design … webs?" Michi glanced at a large one in the tree above them. "Lots of work in Australia for you. I forgot how bloody big the spiders are here."

A shower of cool drops fell on them as Greg bounded back and shook his hair. "What are you two crapping on about?"

"Work," Jake said.

"Did my sister tell you she recycles eyes for a living? Very creepy."

"She did and I'm impressed."

Michi handed Greg a beer. He never needed to be asked. "So how busy are you? I'm here for another week and already going stir-crazy."

"Sorry, but I'm going to be shagging my socks off with the chemist as much as possible all week. I'll make an appearance on New Year's Eve, to say goodbye."

"You're serious? You're ditching me for a pharmacist?"

"Yes, that's right." Her brother sniffed. "Our office is closed until New Year. I've got to make deposits into the sex bank. It's been a very sparse year."

She looked at him in disbelief. "But Josh is flying back to Tokyo tomorrow. Please don't leave me at the mercy of Mum and Dad."

"People have lives, Michi-moooo. They don't stop just because you're gracing us with your biannual visit."

Michi glared at her brother. "Yep, thanks."

Greg looked like he had a great idea. "Hey, you're not working this week, Jake. You should take her out and show her what she's missing."

Michi waved her hand around. "No, definitely not. I'm sure Jake is busy."

"No, I'm not. I was just going to get some surfing in." Jake said. "I've got to make deposits into the *surf* bank."

"See, he's busy surfing," Michi said to Greg.

"He can't fucking surf all day long." Greg turned to Jake. "Can you?"

"Nope. I'd like to take you out, Michi. Repay some of the kindness your family has shown me."

Michi glanced at the Christmas banquet her mother was putting out. "My parents are kind to everyone."

"Don't be a bitch, Mich." Greg slapped his leg. "That rhymes."

Michi wasn't sure if it was the afternoon sun or Jake's stare, but she suddenly felt hot. "Okay, if you're sure it's no bother."

"Are you usually a bother?" Jake said.

She felt cornered and didn't like it. She certainly didn't want Greg to see how flustered Jake was making her. Her brother was a shark. One whiff of blood and he'd attack. "That would be lovely, Jake. Thank you."

Greg seemed relieved to palm his sister off. "Great, it's a date."

Michi looked embarrassed, and Greg burst out laughing. "Fine, you ole prude … it's an appointment."

*

Appointment or not, it felt like a date when Michi rifled through her suitcase the next morning to find something to wear. She always kept things simple. She had to on her salary. But she'd also packed with her parents and their creepy friends in mind, so understated and conservative was the holiday theme—something she was regretting now she was going out with Mr. Sex-on-a-stick. Not that *she* was thinking about having sex with him. She just assumed many women were. Jake had that look about him. Even her brother made no secret of wanting him.

She settled on navy shorts with a white shirt and tan sandals. She didn't need much make-up. Even though she liked to complain about the Aussie sun, she'd enjoyed getting some for a change, and her skin was golden. She looked at herself in the mirror. She jokingly called herself 'Wasian' – half western, half Asian. She knew she was pretty. She was no china doll, though. She was five foot ten and curvy. Plus she had freckles.

She'd been raised in Australia, but she often appeared more Japanese than Australian—certainly more Japanese than her mother. Growing up, she didn't have the laid-back attitude of most of her friends. She was contained, and conservative. Michi favored the Japanese way of not speaking unless there was something meaningful to say. When she was in Australia, she often yearned for Japan, but when she was there, she felt like an alien too. She was always on display there. And she felt like a giant.

She didn't quite know where she fit in, so London was a convenient third option. And she loved it there. Not the weather, but her friends, and work.

She heard the doorbell and her mother's heels clacking across the floor to answer it. She heard her squeal in delight when she saw it was Jake. As usual, her father wasn't far behind, and she could hear him greet Jake like he was a hero returning from war.

Michi suddenly felt sick. What was she doing?

Her mother clearly adored Jake, while her father thought he was a top bloke. And Jake had been brainwashed into liking them.

All excellent reasons to steer clear of him. Besides, she was only here for another week. She didn't need any complications.

It was too late to cancel now, so she would enjoy today and then never lay eyes on him again. Simple. She grabbed her bag and headed out into the hall near the front door.

Jake smiled when he saw her. "Hey, Michi, you look nice."

"Thanks," Michi said with fake nonchalance.

You look drop-dead gorgeous yourself, thought Michi, *but guys like you usually know that*. His hair was tousled, as though he'd just rolled out of bed. In fact, he probably had, with some supermodel or something. He was wearing striped shorts and a navy T-shirt with a …

"Is that an eyeball on your shirt?"

Jake gave her a wink. "Wore it for you."

Michi couldn't help but laugh. "You're lucky I collect corneas and not prostate tissue."

"What are you two young'uns up to today?" Keith asked.

Michi cringed at her father's use of young'uns. "That's Jake's call. He's the local."

"I thought we'd just see how the day pans out. We'll use the force."

"How very Jake Skywalker of you." Michi pretended to be enthusiastic, but preferred it when things were scheduled.

Keith and Kayoko led them to the door. Michi suddenly felt fifteen again.

"Be a good girl," Kayoko advised.

Michi fought the urge to slap her mother and headed for the door. Her mother's idea of being a "good girl" was a little different to hers and usually included sex toys.

Michi ducked her mother's attempt to hug her (Jake wasn't so lucky) and escaped out the door. She noticed Jake's battered old 4WD in the driveway. She was a little surprised. He looked more like a motorbike kind of guy, or at least like he'd drive something slightly pretentious, like a new Jeep.

"Does this thing drive?"

"It did on the way here."

Jake opened the door and Michi climbed in. Then he went round to the driver's side. Michi noticed a bunch of maps shoved between the seats. She flicked her finger over them: New South Wales, Northern Territory, Queensland.

"Do you like driving long distances?"

"I like getting out of the city when I can. I go camping."

"In a tent?"

"That's usually what camping means."

"Did you get the memo about snakes in Australia?" Michi asked.

Jake looked amused. "I did, and I try not to bother them."

"Are you sure you're English? You're a little Crocodile Hunter."

"Born and bred Brit, but I love this place."

"Different strokes for different folks." Michi looked out the window at the Mosman houses. "Where are we going? Skydiving? Shark hunting?"

"Luna Park."

"Luna Park?" *WTF?* "What am I, six?"

"No, but you could do with a dose of childlike joie de vivre."

Michi was shocked. "Are you saying I'm uptight?"

Jake gave her one of his already infuriating shrugs. "I barely know you. Are you?"

"I'm not uptight."

"No problem if you are."

"You'd be a little conservative too, if you grew up with my parents."

"Sure, I get it," Jake said. "That whole teenage rebellion thing. But how old are you now?"

"I'm twenty-eight and I'm not rebelling. This is who I am." Why was she defending herself to this guy?

"I like who you are. I think you're kinda cute."

"Kind of cute?" Michi sniffed. "Now who's acting like a child?"

Half an hour later, after an argument about who was paying (Michi paid for her own ticket—after all, this wasn't a date) they had their wristbands on and Michi had first pick of the rides.

"Let's start with the dodgems," she said. Usually she'd head straight for the carousel, but somehow she didn't think that would go down too well with action man, and she considered the dodgem cars to be quite wild.

"Sure, we'll start tame and work our way up."

Tame? Before long they were hooning around in separate dodgem cars. Michi was doing her best to stay on her own side of the circuit and not hit anyone. Jake seemed to enjoy slamming into everything he could, including Michi's car.

"Back off, Jake," she screamed after the third strike.

Jake roared with laughter. "You're driving like a nanna."

"You're driving like a madman."

"It's a dodgem car, *nanna*."

Michi bit her tongue. Literally. Jake slammed into her, down went her teeth and she could taste blood. Damn him. But the worst was yet to come.

"My choice," Jake announced once they were out of the dodgem pavilion.

Michi glanced toward Coney Island. She could handle that. Instead, Jake grabbed her hand and strode toward the Wild Mouse. Michi wanted to throw up. She hated amusement parks, she hated rides. She wasn't a fan of frightening herself on purpose. Her friends at her book club even teased her about her aversion to dark paranormal romances. Quite simply, Michi didn't like to be taken too far out of her comfort zone.

"Ever been on the Wild Mouse before?" Jake asked.

"Not that I can recall."

"A wild mouse virgin!" Jake shoved her into a carriage.

Naturally Michi thought of Toblerone.

Jake slid into the carriage behind her. "I'll be right here."

"Do I need a safety harness or something?"

"You'll be fine."

Her hands clutched the safety bar as the carriage slowly made its way to the top of the roller-coaster.

Michi glanced over the side of the carriage. "This thing is as old as your car."

"Hope it's maintained better."

The old carriage rattled high along the top of the roller-coaster scaffold.

"Check out that view."

Michi looked out at Sydney Harbour in all its blue-watered sunny glory. It was absolutely magnificent. For just a moment, the carriage paused ... and then they dropped.

"Faaaaaaaaaaaaaaaaaaaaark."

The carriage lurched and rattled its way around the tracks. Michi clutched the bar as her body heaved in one direction then another. She screamed the whole way while Jake sat behind her and laughed. She wasn't sure if he was laughing out of fear or at her.

"Having fun, Michi?" Jake yelled.

He was laughing at her.

Finally the carriage rolled into the station and Michi stumbled out.

"Did you enjoy that?" Jake asked.

"It was great." *Right up there with my last pap smear.*

"Didn't scare you?"

"Not overly."

"Then you must always have that look on your face."

Jake pointed at the screen near the exit showing the photos taken of each carriage. One photo showed Michi, eyes rolled back in her head, tonsils on show as she screamed.

Michi flinched when she saw it. "Not my best angle."

"Shall I buy it for you?"

"No thanks."

"Late Christmas gift?" It was clear Jake enjoyed teasing her.

"Pass."

Jake thought it was hilarious. "You could give it to your dentist in lieu of dental X-rays."

Michi glared at him but Jake just smiled. To her surprise, took her hand and led her out into the main thoroughfare. Once they were through the crowd, he turned to her.

"You could just say you don't like scary rides."

"I don't like scary rides."

"Why not?" Jake asked.

"I don't know. I don't like caramel either. Are you going to interrogate me over that?"

Jake gave her a look of faux horror. "You don't like caramel?"

"I can do the Ferris wheel if you want." It was the best pick of a bad bunch.

Jake took her hand again and they walked toward the ride. Michi didn't like all the hand-holding. What did he mean by it? She knew it was crowded, but surely he knew she was perfectly capable of following him through the crowds without getting lost. It was difficult enough to stay cool in the summer heat without his hand sending pulsating waves of heat up her arm.

Holding hands also meant she wasn't able to put space between them. She could only keep him at arm's length, no further. Occasionally she caught a whiff of his scent. *Male* was the one word that came immediately to mind. Her friend Eva always described her husband as male. She joked about how so many men didn't smell male. They doused themselves in awful aftershave. Or their natural scent wasn't that appealing. She said those men stunk of estrogen. Not literally, but they just weren't *male*. Michi had never really understood what Eva meant until this moment.

Jake was male.

Jake was so male it made Michi a little dizzy. And she didn't like it.

He let go of her hand once they were in line for the Ferris wheel, but that wasn't any better. The line was crowded and she found herself pressed even closer to Jake. Every way she turned, another part of her body was pressed against him. She could barely breathe. So much so that she was relieved to board the carriage—something she'd never felt at an amusement park before.

Once they were floating up toward the sky, Jake spoke. "You cut up dead bodies for a living but you don't like being scared. Why is that?"

"You sound like my roommate Clementine. But I find my work to be … ordered. There's a certain way of dealing with the body and the tissue, and it's the same every time. To me it's just a process that I implement, and if it's successful, it's an opportunity for someone else to regain their sight. It's anything but scary."

"Do you always like things to be *ordered*?"

There was that stare again.

"It's preferable."

"When was the last time you did something that frightened you?"

"Quite frankly, I'm frightened now." Michi turned away from him and looked down at the park below and then out at the Harbour Bridge and Opera House. "The harbor's busy," she said, trying to change the subject.

Jake looked at her in total disbelief. "Christ, you're really a tourist. It's the Sydney to Hobart Yacht Race today. Everyone is out on the water."

She glanced down at the line. "Or on a Ferris wheel."

"You hungry?" he asked.

There was something about his question that unnerved her. In fact, everything about him unnerved her. Michi was self-aware enough to know it wasn't just him. She was like this with anyone who flirted with her. Throw some sexual energy into the mix and suddenly she felt like prey.

Michi had the urge to run, but that would've meant instant death, off the side of the Ferris wheel. She needed to change the dynamic between them. "How about we make a deal?" she asked.

Jake seemed interested. "Okay."

"I'll go on a couple more scary rides with you …"

"Yes?"

"If you stop flirting with me." There, she'd said it.

He clearly had no idea what she was talking about. "I'll be honest, I find you attractive, but I'm pretty sure I'm not flirting with you."

"With respect, guys like you just do it automatically, with anything with a pulse."

"Yes, that was respectful," Jake said sarcastically. He turned away for a moment as if to gather his thoughts. Then he looked back at her.

"There. There it is again. That look," she said.

"That's just my eyes." He crossed them and stared at her.

"That's better." She couldn't help but laugh.

His eyes rolled back in place and he narrowed them slightly. "You work with eyes but you don't see very clearly."

"I see that the way you look at me makes me uncomfortable."

Jake immediately looked apologetic. "Okay, I'm sorry. I don't want you to be uncomfortable around me."

There was an edge in her voice. "Well, I am. I don't know you, but you're looking at me like …"

"Like what?"

Michi could feel a trail of sweat down her back now. "Like you're weighing up what it would be like to kiss me."

Now it was Jake's turn to look unnerved. "What if I am?"

"No offence, Jake, but you seem like the kind of guy that looks at every woman like that."

Jake flinched, as though he'd been slapped. "No offence, Michi, but you seem like the kind of woman who makes broad and inaccurate assumptions."

"It's not going to happen."

"You sure about that?"

"Absolutely. Because I'm about to go on the Rotor with you and that means you back off. That's the deal."

"Fair enough."

Their ride came to an end. Ever the gentleman, Jake took her arm as she stepped off the Ferris wheel, but dropped her hand once she was on solid ground. Then, as they headed toward the Rotor he said, "Do you always choose the safer option?"

*

Ten minutes later, Michi wasn't so sure. She'd started to sweat in the line. By the time their turn came, her legs were shaking. The guy who ran the ride had to pull her onto it, because she was frozen and getting in everyone's way. She now had her eyes squeezed shut but still felt like parts of her were going to fly off. The Rotor was every bit as frightening as Michi expected it to be.

But on the flip side, Jake hadn't touched her since he'd helped her off the Ferris wheel. She kept telling herself that she was relieved, but as she emerged from the Rotor and followed him into Coney Island she couldn't help feeling disappointed. He'd given up easily. Quitter!

"Let's try the Mirror Maze," he called over his shoulder.

Okay, quitter.

Coney Island was packed, with long lines for all the rides, but the Mirror Maze was relatively empty. Michi laughed as she stepped into it and caught sight of herself in dozens of mirrors. Short, fat, tall, each reflection was weirder than the last. They moved from mirror to mirror, laughing and waving their arms around. The maze was lit with strange lights and carnival music played loudly. They were surrounded by dozens of misshapen versions of themselves, and each turn they took was the wrong one.

"Oh shit, my eyes! This one is so unbelievably grotesque," Jake called out.

Michi ran over to him but then saw it was a normal mirror. "You're right, that one's hideous."

He moved on to the next one.

"Check this one out."

Michi doubled over laughing. He was wider than he was tall.

"No wonder you wouldn't kiss me," Jake moaned.

Michi gave him a playful slap. "That was more your attitude than your looks."

Jake grabbed her wrist and pulled her close to him. Very close. Too close. She stopped laughing and stared into his eyes.

"You promised," she said. "If I went on the Rotor, you promised."

"I didn't promise anything. I don't make promises I can't keep."

And with that he kissed her. His lips slammed down on hers. She didn't even bother resisting. She slid her arms up around his neck and responded with ferocious desire. He pushed her back against a mirror, and around them hundred of versions of them kissed like it was the first and last time it would ever happen. Finally, Jake pulled back. His eyes were glazed.

"You're right. That's way more frightening than the Rotor."

Michi turned and ran from the maze.

*

Michi stared out the window at the harbor. Jake had finally caught up to her and brought her to Luna Park's bar, The Deck. He'd put her in a seat by a window and gone to get them both a drink.

She needed one.

What the hell was that kiss? She'd never been kissed like that. She didn't know it was possible to be kissed like that. Oh yes, she read romance books—she had a real soft spot for them—but even in the books she read it wasn't like *that*. She was awash with desire. She could feel the moisture between her legs and knew it wasn't sweat because the bar was air-conditioned. Sitting here now she could barely think straight.

"Here's your beer."

"Thanks."

Jake sat opposite her and watched her for a moment. "You okay?"

"Sure, why wouldn't I be?" she said way too quickly.

"I've wanted to kiss you from the moment I laid eyes on you yesterday."

Christ, they needed to turn up the air conditioning in the bar.

Michi gave him the evil eye. "You make it sound like you deserve a medal for waiting so long."

"And right now," he continued, "I'd like to take you back to my place, but I won't because I don't want to scare you off."

"What makes you think I scare that easily?"

As soon as she'd said it she wished she hadn't. They locked eyes, and there was a moment where he visibly bit his lip ...

and then they both cracked up. As daft as she felt, it broke the tension.

"Yeah, right, you're a regular adrenaline junkie," Jake laughed.

"You must think I'm such a wimp," she said.

"C'mon, with your job? No. You know what I think?" Jake ran his eyes over her face. "I think you like things to have a certain order to them. I bet your apartment is very organized."

"Yes, it is. Drives my roommates mad." Michi squinted slightly. "So what else, Sherlock?"

"You live a life that to most bystanders seems quite interesting, even courageous. You've left your home country, moved to London. You probably travel to Europe when you can."

Michi didn't like where this was heading now. "I do."

"You have a job that is great dinner party conversation and god knows would give me nightmares." He leaned forward. "But you don't want to lose control. Screaming your arse off on a ride feels out of control to you. And I imagine it's the same for you in bed."

There was an intake of breath. "You know, if I wanted a full psychological evaluation, I'd speak to my parents."

"But why would you do that when they're the root of your problem, right?"

"Are you always this rude?"

"You seem to bring it out in me."

"I have no intention of sleeping with you," Michi said.

"Good, because I have no intention of sleeping either."

"I won't fuck you."

"Michi, you said you wouldn't kiss me either."

Michi turned and stared out the window. She yearned for London. She always felt trapped in Sydney and Jake was making it worse.

"Don't you like what you see here?" Jake asked quietly.

"You mean in the view, or in you?" Michi gave him a resigned smile. "Why do people love particular places? Because they're the best version of themselves there, right?"

"I guess that's one reason."

"You like Australia because you get to be all *nature boy*."

Jake looked like he was about to laugh. "That's right, and in fact, I'll be getting my own cartoon soon, *The Adventures of Nature Boy*."

"Make fun of me if you want, but I never had a chance to know or like myself in Sydney," Michi said. "I was raised in a bubble that was very much about my parents. I look at that harbor and remember the yacht we'd spend every New Year's Eve on. Josh, Greg and I would be dressed like dolls, but as the booze flowed, the adults would forget we were there. The things I saw were not appropriate for children."

"I see."

Michi eyed him with defiance. "No, you don't. You look around this city and all you have are the memories you've made here. I look around and have nothing but reminders of a city that made me miserable, reminders of how self-absorbed my parents were."

"Were they that bad?" Jake asked quietly. "They've been so kind to me."

"Of course they have. As people they're warm and welcoming. As parents, they failed to protect me." Michi finished her drink. "Probably best you take me home."

*

Jake pulled up outside Keith and Kayoko's house. The drive had been silent. He put the old car into park and turned to her.

"I've been invited to your parents' New Year's party on the boat. But I don't have to come."

"I don't have a problem if you're there." She did, but she'd never admit it.

"I apologize if I stepped over a line with you today."

"This isn't about you, Jake. It's about me and this place."

"What if spending time with me could change that?"

Michi raised an eyebrow.

"I don't mean it like that," Jake said sheepishly. "The thing is I love this place. Not just Sydney but the whole bloody country. Let me share that with you."

"In a week? The whole of Australia?"

"Not the whole country. Let me share a little bit. And maybe then you'll go back *home* to London with some fond memories."

"I'm not interested in a fling."

"We won't have one. Let's hang out together, as friends. It's less complicated anyway."

Michi thought about this for a moment. The idea was appealing. When he wasn't flirting with her, she enjoyed Jake's company. And hanging out with him would get her out of the house.

"Okay, why not. Show me your Australia."

"Great, I'll pick you up at six in the morning. Pack for an overnight road trip. Nothing fancy."

Michi baulked. "I thought you meant you'd take me ... I don't know, to the zoo or something."

"You want to see animals, I'll show you animals. You're not backing out now, are you?"

Michi quite liked the idea of a couple of days away. Her parents were already doing her head in. "I'll see you at six." She swung herself out of the car. "By the way, Jake, when you apologized to me before, thank you for saying sorry you kissed me."

Jake reached over to the door. "I apologized for crossing a line. I'm not sorry for kissing you." He slammed the door shut and backed out of the driveway.

＊

Jake pulled up right on six. He was evidently a stickler for punctuality, thought Michi. And she approved. She'd been raised by people who figured nothing started until they arrived, so punctuality was a foreign concept. Michi herself was one of those rare members of her generation who wore a watch.

She allowed Jake to carry her bag to the car, although she did protest all the way, and then she pretended she didn't see her parents, who were standing on their bedroom balcony waving them off. A few minutes later they were on the Pacific Highway heading north, away from the city.

"There's a map next to you I've marked the route on," Jake said.

Michi was impressed. He'd marked this one up for her benefit. His other maps weren't marked.

Michi read the map for a moment. "Oh ... we're heading south?"

"The map's upside down."

Michi turned the map around. "I knew that." She studied it for a few minutes and then neatly folded it back up. "Excellent. I've never heard of the place we're going, but I've got my bearings. Thank you."

"No problem." They were at a red light so Jake quickly set up his iPod and the car filled with music.

"Do we need to stop for supplies?"

"I've got everything," Jake said.

"I'll give you some money."

"No need."

Michi's eyes flashed angrily. "I'm paying my own way."

"Okay, settle down. You can put some petrol in at some stage."

That appeased her. "Thank you."

They turned right at Wahroonga onto the freeway and merged with the traffic.

"It's less than an hour from here," Jake said.

"Why'd you pick me up so early then?"

"We needed to get on here before the holiday traffic. By nine it's nuts." He concentrated while he overtook one of the mammoth trucks that ruled the Australian roads. "Besides, where we're going, you'll want a full day."

"Fair enough." Michi relaxed back. "Have you always enjoyed camping?"

"God, no. My parents took us on holidays to resorts in Spain. The closest I ever got to any animals were the other brats in the Kids' Clubs." Jake threw her a sideways glance. "I followed a girl to Australia. Phoebe's family were big on camping." He looked almost sad for a moment. "I got on well with her dad. He taught me how to appreciate it."

Michi felt a stab of jealousy, which was ridiculous, she knew. "What happened to the girl?"

A shadow crossed Jake's eyes. "Just didn't work out, but I have this to thank her for." He waved his arm around his 4WD. "I've been in Australia for three years. I love it."

"When are you planning to go home?"

"When are you?"

"Touché."

The further away from Sydney they got, the more relaxed they were. No surprise, but Jake was great company. He was funny, and fun, telling tall tales about his adventures, and making up weird road games.

"Number plate sentences. I'll go first. EDB." He pointed at the number plate of the car in front of them. "Every dog burps."

"Nice one," laughed Michi. "My turn. PMT ..." She looked mortified.

"That one speaks for itself."

And the two of them cracked up.

The trip flew by and suddenly they were off the freeway and heading past the villages of the Central Coast toward Bouddi National Park. Part of the road was unsealed, and Michi finally appreciated the beast that Jake called a car. She was thrown around in a similar fashion to when she was on the Wild Mouse, but hopefully without the drop at the end. Eventually, he pulled off the road, parked the beast and they jumped out.

Jake began unloading the car. "It's a bit of a hike and we have to carry everything."

"Isn't there a porter?"

"It's his day off." He handed her a trolley. "That's not just any trolley. It's like the 4WD of trolleys. It handles rough terrain."

They loaded the trolley up with supplies, hoicked some backpacks on, and last but not least Jake shoved his surfboard under his arm. Then Michi gestured for Jake to take the lead.

"After you." She watched him walk off. "You can deal with the snakes first."

"The first person scares the snake," Jake called over his shoulder. "The second person gets the bite."

"Thanks, Bear Grylls." Michi's eyes darted around.

It was not quite 8 am but it was already hot, and the flies were out. It was difficult to swoosh them away when your arms were loaded with supplies. Michi had to make do with blowing them away using air from her mouth. There were a couple of moments when lounging by her parents' pool was suddenly appealing.

It took about fifteen minutes to reach the campground, but it was worth it. It was a pristine stretch of land leading right onto the beach. There was a barbecue and a toilet, and two other tents set up, but other than that, picturesque wilderness as far as the eye could see.

"What do you think?" Jake beamed at her, visibly thrilled to get back to nature.

"It's great." Then Michi pretended to be worried. "No yowies?" She wondered if he knew about Australia's version of Big Foot – perhaps she could have some fun and convince him the mythical beasts were real.

"None sighted since July."

Damn.

Jake led her over to the far corner of the campground, away from the other tents. Finally, they dumped their stuff. Jake clapped his hands together—down to work.

"Right, where's your tent?"

"My what?"

"So, did you bring a tent?"

Michi looked confused. "Was I meant to?"

"Well, we're camping, so yes." Jake gave a wicked laugh. "You can share my tent."

Michi immediately jumped into attack mode. "Listen, I've already told you—"

"Settle down, Michi, you'll scare the wildlife away." Jake tossed her a large pack. "There's your tent."

And with that he turned and set up his own—in what would have to be record time, thought Michi. She'd never seen anything like it. If Armageddon hit and they all had to survive in the wild, she wanted Jake on her team. Meanwhile she was still laying her tent out flat and trying to work out where the poles went.

"Want some help?" called Jake.

"No, all good thanks."

Jake tidied up the rest of the gear, pulled out a wetsuit and stripped.

Holy mother of god, thought Michi. He's freaking hot! He had Speedos on, but other than that she got a good look at every muscle, every golden brown ripple, and every bulge. By the time he zipped his wetsuit up, Michi was completely flustered and ready for a cold plunge herself.

"Stupid bloody tent." She let him know she was concentrating on the tent poles.

"I'm gonna hit the waves. See you in a while."

"Great. Enjoy." Michi stood and watched him run down to the beach, board under his arm. "Oh. My. Gawd."

Then she turned back to the tent. "Right, you bastard. I'm going to conquer you if it's the last thing I do."

*

And conquer it she did. By the time Jake returned from the beach her tent was up, she'd set up the canvas camp chairs and had the billy on for a cup of tea.

"Wow, I'm impressed." He meant it too.

"Wasn't that difficult," Michi lied. She'd worked out Rubik's cubes with more ease.

"It has a bit of a tilt to it," Jake pointed out.

Michi waved off his concerns. "It adds character."

She pretended to ignore him while he ripped off the wetsuit and wrapped a towel around his waist. The guy was built. If she was the type of woman who was interested in casual flings, she'd seriously consider it. But she wasn't, so it was out of the question. Still, the barometer definitely rose each time he took off his shirt.

Jake sipped the tea Michi handed him. "I thought I'd take you on a coastal walk. There are some amazing Aboriginal sites around here."

"Is Bouddi a local Aboriginal word?"

"It means both *water breaking over rocks* and *heart*."

"It's both of those." Michi surveyed the landscape. "How do you know so much about Aboriginal history?"

Jake shrugged. "The more connected I feel to this land, the more I want to understand the Traditional Owners. For instance, we're currently standing on Darkinjung land. You can't connect to this place without recognizing that the Darkinjung are not only the Traditional Owners … they are this place." He stomped his foot on the earth. "They're this."

Jake threw on shorts and a T-shirt. "Come on, let's go for a hike. I want you to get a feel for the area." He looked her up and down for a second. "Put on a hat. I don't want you to get burned." He tapped his own nose with one finger. "Although your freckles are gorgeous."

*

Michi couldn't ever remember such a glorious day. The sun beat down on them, there were insects galore, but the scenery was spectacular, with jaw-dropping ocean views, sheer cliffs, sandstone boulders and the trails through the ancient forest. Jake pointed out unusual plants, and a couple of bush turkey nests. At one point he held out his arm to stop her, and she noticed a snake slither into the bush.

"Not venomous," he assured her.

It turned out he was also a certified bird nerd, and knew the names of many of the one hundred and fifty species of birds the area was home to.

"Some are real jetsetters," he joked. "They fly in from New Guinea for the summer."

But the highlight was undoubtedly the Aboriginal rock engravings and charcoal drawings. Michi stood there in awe of the ancient markings. She wanted to place her hands on them, but Jake stopped her, explaining that they needed to respect them, and not touch.

"How old do you think they are, Jake?"

"I don't know. I've read that other carvings in this region are only about five thousand years old, so probably a similar age."

"Only five thousand?" Michi couldn't even begin to comprehend how long that was.

"Quite young, when you think that Aborigines have been living here for at least forty thousand years. Shits all over some of the historical sights you line up for in Europe." He stared at the markings. "And still people just don't get it."

Michi could see that baffled him. When put like that, in this place, it baffled her too. And on some level, it shamed her. It took an Englishman to open her eyes to this. The irony was not lost on her.

Michi spoke quietly. "I feel embarrassed. I barely know anything about the people who lived here."

"Just start at the beginning."

"And what's that mean, Jake?"

"Respect where you're standing."

*

It was beer o'clock back at the campground. Michi went for a swim to cool off, and then joined Jake in a canvas chair, with a beer in hand and an amazing view. She leaned back and let the last rays of the afternoon sun warm her face.

"What a great day." She looked across at him. "Thank you so much for bringing me here."

"I love the place, so I'm happy to share."

"Do you feel this way about your own country, Jake?"

He thought about this for a moment. "Sure I do, sometimes. The last few times I've been back I've gone camping, much to my parents' horror. And I've got to say, parts of Britain are truly impressive. But there's something about this country ... It's bloody harsh, and yet it's familiar to me." He sighed and looked up. "I love the sky. It's so vast. You're very lucky to have grown up in such an open place."

"Yeah, Mosman in the nineties was open, all right."

"Now you sound like a Pom," Jake laughed. "Stop whining, will you? I'm going to make you dinner."

They had a barbecue dinner of steak and salad, followed by cupcakes and wine as the sun went down.

"I'm impressed with the feed. You're like the king of camping, Jake."

"King of Camping is my other nickname, right after Nature Boy." Jake cracked open a bottle of wine and poured her a glass.

"You've outdone yourself. The plastic wineglass is a nice touch."

"You like it? I put a lot of thought into it."

"Do you take a lot of girls camping?"

Jake pulled a face. "God no." He looked at her serious all of a sudden. "I used to go camping with Phoebe, my ex. But other than her ... this is my thing, my time. If I bring someone with me I want that person to add to the experience."

Michi gulped her wine. "That's a lot of pressure. I hope I've added something."

Jake smiled, light again. "I've enjoyed having a laugh at your tent-pitching skills."

"So I'm like the camping comedy channel?"

"Yep." He pretended to remember something. "Oh and I did like the way your bottom swayed from side to side as you walked up that hill this morning."

Michi tossed back some more wine, horrified at the thought of him watching her bum. "That's me, a laugh-a-minute arse swayer."

Jake reached over and switched off the lamps. "Easier to stargaze," he explained.

And that's what they did. They talked and laughed and looked at the stars until late into the night. The night sky was dazzling. At times Michi was certain she could put her hand up and pluck a star from it.

"You know, Aborigines were practicing astronomy long before the Greeks. If you look up there, you can see an emu." Jake's finger traced the sky.

"An emu?" Michi squinted a bit. "Nope—I can see the Southern Cross, though."

"Its head is at the bottom left-hand corner of the Southern Cross," Jake explained. "Then it stretches out into the galaxy."

"An emu?"

"There's an Aboriginal legend about a blind man who used to send his wife out to collect food. One day she didn't return home, so he went to find her. He discovered her body. A giant emu had killed her. Anyway, the blind man speared the emu and sent it up into the Milky Way, where we can still see it tonight."

"Unlike the blind man," Michi said.

"Yes, I was never sure how he saw that emu." Jake shrugged as if the answers to these things weren't important. "There are countless ways to see things. What's it mean to see something, anyway?"

"It means a lot to those people who get the cornea transplant."

"I have no doubt," said Jake. "Sight is a sense I would hate to lose. But *to see*, well that's rather subjective."

"In what way?"

"A perfect example is how this country moves me and you to see something very different in it." Jake swiveled in his chair a bit.

"I've seen it differently today," Michi admitted. "With you."

"Perhaps truly seeing is the ability to see things through the eyes of others."

They locked eyes. He looked like he was about to reach out for her. She certainly wanted to kiss him. Or more. She remembered the kiss at Luna Park and her body flooded with heat. A shadow crossed his impossibly handsome face, and he seemed to retreat again.

"I'm crapping on," he said. "It's the wine."

"I think it's time to go to bed, Jake."

His eyes lit up. "I thought you'd never ask."

Michi just rolled her eyes and made her way into her own tent. "Night, Jake," she called.

"Night, Michi."

Michi lay awake in her tent for a long time. Eventually, she could hear Jake unzip his own tent and climb in. It was silent outside. Or as silent as the Australian bush could be. There were cicadas, and other insects buzzing around. In the distance she could hear a lyrebird screaming. Either that or it was a woman being attacked, probably by a yowie. Something scratched outside.

Something scratched outside?

Michi sprung upright. She could hear something snuffling. Something was out there. Something large by the sounds it was making. She could hear it plodding around the tent. What the hell was it? Did they have wild pigs around here? What if it was a yowie?

"Shoo," Michi hissed. "Pssst."

Something hit the side of her tent.

"Jake!"

And then the whole tent collapsed on top of her.

"JAAAAAKE!"

She heard him come running. "Michi, Jesus, what the fuck?"

Michi flailed around while Jake yanked at her tent and lifted it off her so she could crawl out. She swung around, trying to see in the darkness. What if that thing was still nearby?

"Something was sniffing around my tent. It knocked it over."

"It *was* hanging by a thread."

"Listen, I don't know if there are mountain lions out here—"

Jake threw his head back and laughed. "Or drop bears."

Michi eyeballed him. "You don't believe me?"

"I just think it's your way of getting to sleep in my tent."

Michi looked horrified at the thought. "I'm not sleeping with you."

"Listen, there's no way we can put that bloody thing back up with nothing but this torch."

He had a point. "Perhaps if you shine it there I can find the pegs."

Jake laughed at her. "Michi, don't be daft. Come into my tent. I'm the lesser of two evils." He leaned in close. "I did hear something out here."

Michi was in Jake's tent like a shot. Jake grabbed some of her bedding and dragged it in with him.

"Here, you'll need this."

"Thanks." She lay her bedding out next to his.

Jake crawled back onto his mat and drew the light camp sheet over himself. "Just try and keep your hands to yourself, Michi."

"I'll do my best, Jake. Goodnight."

And as much as she thought she'd never fall asleep, she was sound asleep in minutes.

*

The next morning Michi woke before Jake. She stared at him, sound asleep. He had endless lashes. There was no doubt that he'd backed off since Luna Park and been nothing but a gentleman and a friend since. She was glad, although part of her still wished he'd kiss her again. Chemistry like that didn't come around often. She was almost temped to wake him and explore that chemistry. After all, a few more days and she'd never have to see him again. But deep down, she knew that was something that scared her.

She crawled out of the tent. The morning was silent, apart from the crashing waves. It was already warm and the sky was bathed in the most stunning golden light. She paused near the flap of the tent when she saw three kangaroos grazing nearby. She didn't want to scare them, so moved very quietly toward her bag, pulled out her phone, and took a photo. She added a message. *My morning view. BTW did you get flowers for Paige?* Then she pressed send to both her roommates, Clementine and Debra.

Next, she forwarded the same photo to Paige, this time with a text. *I'm thinking of you today. I'm sending love.*

Jake woke, and emerged from the tent looking tousled and sexy.

"That was quite a night," he said with a wink.

She watched him pull on his wetsuit again from behind her dark glasses. He swung around and caught her.

"You okay?"

"Just checking out the view," she said.

She walked down to the beach with him and went for a swim, although she waited until he was well out in the waves to take her sundress off. The water was sublime. She dove under a wave and emerged completely refreshed. She heard a whistle, and saw Jake was waving at her. Then, he pointed at something. To her complete delight, there was a pod of about six dolphins riding the waves a little further out.

"Oh my god!" Michi shrieked. "Oh wow!" She clapped her hands and jumped up and down, and swam toward them for a closer look.

Afterward, they emerged from the ocean together, and Michi felt freer than she had in a long time. Perhaps ever. She didn't even care that she was standing on the beach with Jake in nothing but her bikini.

"I wish we could stay another day," Michi said.

"You're only here for a short time, and your parents would kill me if you spent most of it here."

Michi gave him a look that said being killed by her parents was a more appealing option than returning to Sydney today. "One more day?"

"They've done the right thing by me. So I'm doing the same for them. You're going home." He softened slightly. "But let's hang out in Sydney too, okay?"

"I bet there won't be dolphins."

"I'll find some for you at Bondi."

They lugged everything back to the car, and once it was loaded headed back toward the freeway. Michi wished they'd gone on a much longer road trip. She found herself wanting this one to never end. Jake entertained her with a hair-raising tale about breaking down in the middle of the Northern Territory, half a day from anywhere. She told him about the first time she ever harvested corneas from a body. She felt like she wanted to talk to him forever. But all talk stopped the moment they drove up her parents' street and she noticed a black Mercedes parked in the driveway. Her whole body tensed, and Jake sensed it immediately.

"Michi, what's wrong?"

"Keep driving."

"What do you mean?"

"Keep driving!" she snapped.

Jake drove past Keith and Kayoko's house and Michi watched as a large man with gray hair got out of the Mercedes and walked toward her parents' house.

"Take me back to your place, Jake," Michi said stone-faced.

"Who is he?"

"No one I want to see."

Michi turned her head and watched the north shore slip by as Jake drove her back to his place in Bondi.

*

Jake lived in a lovely little two-bed apartment on Beach Road, about five minutes' walk from Bondi Beach. It was sunny and airy, with steps down from the kitchen to a shared garden.

The flat was filled with large comfortable couches and bright rugs and cushions. There were some black-and-white framed photos on the walls, and the fridge was plastered with more photos.

"Who else lives here?" Michi looked around at what was definitely a woman's touch.

"I came to stay with a mate's sister when I first arrived. Just for a week. During that week, her other roommate met a bloke and bailed on her. So I took the room. I've claimed Libby as my own sister now. I love her."

"Is she here?"

"No, you probably passed her at the airport. She's gone back to the UK for a couple of weeks." Jake smiled kindly. "You can have her room. She won't mind."

"Thanks. I appreciate it."

Jake looked as though he wanted to ask more questions, but held back. Instead, he kept things light, and kept Michi laughing, which she appreciated.

They ate dinner at a Thai place down the road, and then went for a walk along the beach. Even at night, Bondi was busy, but incredibly beautiful in its own colorful way. Both the north and south ends twinkled with lights from the houses. The pavilion sat in the middle of the promenade like the heart of it all. Michi hadn't been to Sydney's eastern suburbs for years. She'd forgotten how much she liked the area.

They stopped at a beachside bar and took an outside table. Michi checked her phone while Jake went inside to grab some drinks. Four missed calls and two texts. The first one was from Clementine.

I'm back home, got an early flight to be here for Paige. I sorted the flowers too. Also I have HUGE news. But will save it until you're here. Can't wait.

No doubt something to do with moving to New York to be with Sam, thought Michi.

And then, a text from her father.

Where are you, moo moo?

Michi quickly texted back: *Still camping. Shit coverage here. Xo*

A few seconds later he replied.

Okay, honey. Have fun. But remember we've got our NYE cruise.

Michi turned her phone off. She wished she were back in London, away from her parents. But then she spotted Jake carrying two seriously garish cocktails and she felt torn.

"I got us something a bit schmancy." He plunked the glasses down on the table.

"They look like something I'd drink at Club Med."

"I know, the bartender thought I was a complete dork when I ordered them. But hey, what he thinks of me is none of my business, right?"

"Right." Michi held her glass up. "To not caring what others think." She took a long sip through the straw and then reeled back. "What's in that?"

"I don't know. Vodka, rum, some weird happy liquor."

"Are you trying to get me drunk so you can take advantage of me?"

"Pretending to be a wild pig didn't work."

"Was that you?"

Jake put his hands up in a "don't shoot" pose. "I'm joking. It wasn't me. No idea what it was." And then he grinned. "But I'd like to meet it one day and shake its paw. I liked having you in my tent."

Michi laughed and then sipped her drink. "God, this is great."

"The view helps."

"I love it. It's busy, though. Doesn't Bondi do your head in?"

"No, I get to work and surf. And when I need to get away from it all, I do. Pretty simple." He watched her for a moment.

"Michi, what are we going to do about your parents? I don't want to lie to them."

"I just need a day to clear my head and then I'll go back." She leaned across the table. "Don't you want me around?"

"I'm enjoying every minute of it. It's just I know how much they were looking forward to your visit."

"Then they should focus on me and stop having other visitors."

Jake watched her carefully. "Who was that man?"

Michi shook her head. "Doug. He's a friend of my father's."

"Yeah, but what did he do to you?"

*

Michi woke. The party up on deck was so noisy. That wasn't unusual. Her parents always had noisy parties, but she usually slept through them. She'd learned that that was the best way for them to be over with quickly. Michi didn't like it when her parents had parties. All the adults pretended to be nice to her when they first arrived, but then they'd get drunk, and they'd ignore her, or even worse, say stupid things to her.

"Owwww, aren't you a little cutie doll … come here and give Aunty Margot/Sam/Roz/Tanya a kiss."

They scared her. Michi preferred it when the adults got so drunk they didn't see her.

Michi needed to do a wee. She lay in her bed and willed herself to go back to sleep, but couldn't. She didn't want to wet the bed. She was a big girl. She didn't do that anymore.

The rocking of the boat made it worse. She could hear the slapping of waves against the side. She got up and tiptoed to the door. She opened it a crack. There was no one there. She slipped out and ran along the corridor toward the bathroom. She could hear music and laughter on deck. She heard a moan in her parents' room, like someone was being hurt. She ran to the door. It was open. She peered through. And then she saw him. Her daddy's friend Doug was moving back and forward behind her own mother, who was kneeling on all fours on the bed. They were both naked. As was Michi's father, who sat on a chair watching them.

Doug turned. He noticed Michi. He didn't stop. He didn't say anything. He just smiled at her.

Michi ran back to her room before her parents saw her, wetting her pants on the way.

*

Jake didn't say anything for a long time. Finally he spoke. "And you've never told your parents?"

Michi shook her head. "Why would I? They thought their behavior was appropriate. By the time I was old enough to realize it wasn't … the moment had passed."

"But if they knew—"

"They'd what? Replace what they took from me that night?"

"You need to discuss this with them," Jake said.

"I'd prefer to just forget the whole thing."

"But you haven't."

Michi was immovable. "I've dealt with this my own way."

"By living in London," Jake said.

"Yes." She stared straight at him. "My father is a shrink. He'd have a field day with this shit. That's not what I want."

"What do you want?"

"I want now what I wanted then: to feel safe." She looked him in the eye, a mixture of defiance and shame. "Boring, eh? I'm not very cool, am I?"

Jake stood and held out his hand. "Come on, I'll take you home."

And they walked back to his place hand in hand.

*

Michi spent the next two days exploring Bondi with Jake. They ate every meal out on the bustling sidewalk cafes and restaurants. She got caught up in the local coffee culture, and dragged Jake in search of the perfect brew. She walked along the coastal pathways from Bondi to Bronte beach while Jake went for a surf. The view was gorgeous and at one point she spotted a pod of dolphins. She smiled—Jake had been right. She felt happier than she had in a long time and could see herself doing the walk daily, if she lived in the area.

If she lived in the area?

Jake had gotten under her skin. She enjoyed his company immensely. The easy rhythm they'd fallen into was weaving its spell. Oh, the spark was there. She could feel the heat between them. And the Luna Park kiss was never far from her mind. But Jake seemed to sense her need for space, and never again crossed the line. Which made her both admire and curse him.

Jake broached the subject of her parents a couple of times, but never pushed it further until dinner on the second night.

"I don't like keeping your whereabouts from your parents."

Michi tried to keep things light. "You've got to choose sides, Jake."

Jake wasn't in the mood for light. "That would be difficult."

Michi was surprised by this. "Why?"

"Your parents helped me through a rough time."

"How nice of them," Michi sniped.

"Mich, I'm not diminishing what happened to you, but give them the opportunity to take responsibility for that."

Michi motioned the waiter for the check. "I'll think about it."

But it was obvious she wasn't going to.

*

Michi woke early on New Year's Eve to voices and immediately knew the day could only go downhill from here.

Her parents were there.

She got dressed and joined them.

Kayoko jumped up from the lounge to hug her daughter. "Hello, darling. How was camping?"

"It was great, thanks." She turned to Jake. "What's going on?"

Keith gave Jake an affectionate nod. "Jake called us."

Michi gave him a look that said, *you traitor.* "Did he now?"

Jake stood, completely unapologetic. "Life's too short, Michi." And with that he left.

Michi wanted to roar after him and kick the crap out of him for doing this to her. Instead, she had to listen as her father pleaded with her.

"Your mother and I have been hurt by the distance you've put between us."

"That distance between us is nothing new, Dad."

"I know that, Michi. But it's been particularly noticeable this time." Keith had an edge to his voice. "Jake has explained to us why it's there."

Kayoko looked like she was about to cry.

Michi thought she'd implode with rage. She couldn't believe Jake had betrayed her like this.

Keith stood and walked over to his daughter. "I had no idea, Moo." He was close to tears. "An apology isn't sufficient. Your mother and I ... we've lived a certain way that might not be conventional, but it works for us." He took a deep breath. "But if I'd know the impact it was having on you."

"How could you not know?"

Keith paled. "I don't know, Moo. I should've. I missed it."
He reached for her hand but she stepped back. "We can work
through this."

"I'm not your fucking patient. I'm your daughter."

Keith changed tack. "We'll get someone else to work with
us on this. One of my colleagues—"

Michi flew off the handle. "I don't want to be in therapy
with you. I don't want to be analyzed. I don't want someone
digging inside my head. That's all bullshit."

Keith was distraught. "What do you want?"

"Parent who are grown-ups," sneered Michi. "I want what
I've never had."

She desperately wanted to grab something and smash it.
But she couldn't. Nothing here belonged to her. She was a
stranger here, in this home, with these people. In the whole
bloody country.

"And all I can ask ..." Keith's voice cracked. "All I can ask ..."

And that was it. Her father broke down sobbing. Michi
was mortified.

Kayoko placed a comforting arm around Keith. "Your
father is asking forgiveness. We both are."

Michi wanted to run. "It's okay. I forgive you. No one ever
touched me."

"Not physically. But your spirit." Keith looked at her, eyes
filled with grief as well as tears. "You were a little girl. And
we took something from you."

There was a ringing in her ears. "I don't want to do this."

"You've got no choice," Kayoko snapped. "You have to
give us a chance."

Michi looked down at her shoes. And with that she started
to cry. And cry. She sat down on the sofa with one parent either
side of her while she sobbed and sobbed. And they held her.
It took a long time, but eventually she stopped. She couldn't
remember the last time she'd cried in front of her parents.

Or the last time they'd just sat there and comforted her, and not analyzed her.

And certainly she couldn't ever remember them taking responsibility for their actions or her pain.

"Spend time with us, Michi. Let's get to know each other again. You might see us differently."

Michi saw the shattered look in their eyes. She was stuck. There was no turning back, but to move forward would take a giant leap.

"Spend New Year with us." Kayoko was stroking her daughter's arm. "We canceled our party."

"I bet there's a few swingers who are sad about that," Michi said.

Kayoko surprised Michi by losing her temper. "Your father and I messed up, Michiko, and we are so very very sorry. We were blind to what happened to you. But you're just as blind to us now."

Michi reeled back. "That's not true."

"No? So you know that your father and I are retiring?"

Michi didn't know that.

"And you know your father had his prostate out. Cancer!"

Michi felt like she'd been kicked in the guts.

Keith put his arm out and comforted his wife. "Kay, honey, we weren't going to say anything." Then he turned to Michi. "It's all good. My tests have been okay."

Kayoko hadn't finished. "Did you know that I love your father? Love him? Totally?"

Michi shook her head.

"I'm so sorry that the way we express that affected you, Michiko." Kayoko's tone softened. "Let us make this up to you. If you knew us better ..."

Michi stared down at her bare feet. "I'll come tonight."

Keith looked ecstatic. "It'll just be us, Greg and a chemist friend of his, and you and Jake."

"Jake's a nice man. I love him," Kayoko said.

Michi rolled her eyes. Old habits die hard.

"And your mother and I have been talking. We're going to come to London, and spend some time with you."

"You don't have to," Michi said as she thought of other places she could move to.

Her parents were looking at her like she was about to evaporate. She hadn't spent time with them, and was leaving tomorrow. "Let's just start with the New Year together, okay?"

"It's a good sign," Kayoko said, obviously thrilled.

Keith and Kayoko stood to leave. They hugged her, numerous times, and she promised to be over at their place by six. She was tempted to leave with them, but she needed to think about what had just happened.

And she wanted to confront Jake.

She didn't have to wait long. He entered not long after her parents left, which made her think he'd simply been waiting outside. He looked prepared for battle.

She pounced immediately. "How the hell could you betray me?"

"Your parents have been good to me. They deserve the opportunity to make amends before you take off again."

"Says who? You? What gives you the right to meddle in this?"

"What gives anyone the right to meddle in anything? Sometimes you just have to do it."

She sneered at him. "Why the fuck are you such a fan anyway?"

"Oh grow up, Michi. I've told you how I feel about them. But it's more than that. I owe them."

This surprised her. "In what way?"

Jake's jaw tensed. "The girlfriend I followed to Australia …"

"Camping Phoebe?"

Jake smiled slightly. "Yeah. Well, her dad and I were ..."
Jake visibly pulled himself together. "We were real close.
He said I was the son he never had. I certainly loved him.
Anyway, Phoebe could be a bit ... headstrong. It's why I loved
her. But one night she had a massive barney with her father.
A dreadful fight. He called me, asking me to intervene, so I
did. I asked her to talk to her father, to clear the air. She didn't
want to. So I didn't push it. With some women you choose
your battles."

Michi didn't say anything, even though she felt that was a
dig at her.

"So I let it go," Jake continued. "I took the easy way out.
I figured it would blow over in a couple of days. But the
next night, we got a call. A heart attack. He died before the
ambulance arrived."

"That's awful," Michi said.

"It was. Phoebe and I couldn't survive that one. She was
devastated that her final words to her father were in anger.
And I'll always regret not pushing for them to resolve their
differences. He loved his daughter. It didn't matter what the
argument was about." Jake ran his fingers through his hair.
"The day after the funeral, Greg took me over to your
parents' place for dinner. I was in a very dark place. They
recognized that and were supportive, that night and for a long
time afterward."

Michi got it. She understood. She was still angry, but she
now knew why he'd called them. "You know where your
loyalty lies."

"You still don't get it do you, you ditzy cow?"

"I get it, life's too short. You learned that the hard way."

"My loyalty is to you. Your dad's been battling cancer, Michi.
You need to sort this out or you'll never forgive yourself."

Michi hadn't even begun to absorb the news about her
father's illness.

Jake took one step toward her. "And I never want to regret failing another woman I love."

"Love?" Now Michi was really confused.

"Michi, I know you're leaving. I know you're not interested in me. But I fell head over heels for you the moment I saw you on Christmas Day in that big fucking hat."

"You didn't like my hat?"

"That's what you take out of that sentence?"

"You're in love with me?" Michi asked quietly.

"Yep."

"That's ridiculous."

Jake ran his fingers through his hair. "Tell me about it."

One more step toward her and then he stopped again. She knew he was never going to cross that line with her. So she crossed it for him. Slowly. She stepped up to him. He was stunned for just a moment, but then he scooped her up and kissed her.

"Michi, I want you, but not now. Not after that today."

She nodded, her eyes glazed with desire. It would happen.

But for now, she was happy to hold him. To be held. Another memory of Sydney she'd cling to on the flight back to London.

*

The *Sakura* was a beautiful boat. Classy, despite the debauchery it had seen, it remained slightly above it all. Michi sat back on deck, happier than she'd felt in a long time. The harbor was busy around them, with hundreds of boats all vying for the prime spots to watch the fireworks. The *Sakura* had a wonderful view of the bridge and the Opera House.

Greg was entertaining everyone, as usual. He was happy, and madly in love. His new boyfriend Hong, the chemist, was delightful, and very laid-back. He didn't blink an eye at Greg's outrageous behavior, even when he kept telling everyone that Hong was well-hong.

Keith and Kayoko were as touchy-feely and as loving as always, and Michi realized it was not and never had been an act. They adored each other. She'd never understand how they could have sex with other people. In fact, that was an even bigger question for her than how they could do what they did to their kids. How did they allow others into that thing that they shared? It was impossible for her to understand. She couldn't bear the thought of Jake being with anyone else. And they hadn't even done the deed yet. But they would, of that she was sure.

Michi looked across the deck at him, and he winked back. She knew she had to get on that plane tomorrow. She had work. She had a life in London.

But he was here.

"Quick, everyone, the countdown." Kayoko clapped her hands excitedly.

Boats all over the harbor had their radios blaring. The countdown began. Ten, nine, eight …

They all moved to the bow of the boat.

Three, two, one. Bang!

Happy New Year!

Thousands of lights exploded above them. Jake pulled Michi into his arms and kissed her. Deep, hot and totally leg-melting.

It was a new year now and what she did with it was up to her. Her brother put his arms around her and Jake, and then her parents did too. They huddled together as a group, heads tilted upward toward the Harbour Bridge, which was illumin-ated with fireworks. It looked beautiful. She could see it now.

And there was no place she'd rather be.

Clementine

Two days before Christmas

Clementine handed the woman the Christmas book bag. "I'm sure your nephew will love it. Boys that age love the Bella & Burton's Misadventures series. We sell a lot of them."

"Thanks. You saved my arse. I never know what to get him." The woman gave her a huge smile and headed for the door. Just as she walked out, Paige rushed in, with Sadie hot on her heels.

"Clem, I've got to go away for the night, so Sadie is going to help out."

Sadie was obviously thrilled to be asked. "You can show me the ropes, sweetie."

"I will." Clementine loved the idea of having Sadie around. They knew each other from the book club, but Clementine had always been a little in awe of her. Sadie was sexy and energetic, always good for a cracking one-liner and a laugh. But she also seemed a little lonely. Probably because she was a single mum, thought Clementine. It meant when she had the opportunity to talk to other adults, she grabbed it with both hands.

Clementine turned back to Paige.

"Anything wrong?" She noticed Paige had an overnight bag.

"Just some family stuff that's come up."

"Are you sure you don't need me tomorrow? Christmas Eve is always busy?"

Paige reached out and patted Clementine's arm. "No, honey, I'll be back early."

Sadie piped in. "And I'm around."

"You have to go to Spain, Clem," Paige said.

Clementine gave the others a guilty look. "I've changed my plans."

"You're not going to *New York*?" Paige asked quietly.

Clementine simply nodded, but looked thrilled all the same.

"Clem!"

Sadie looked impressed. "You go, girl."

Paige wasn't so impressed. "Don't encourage her, Sadie."

Clementine was unapologetic. "It was a last-minute decision but feels right."

Paige was visibly worried. "I don't want to be a spoilsport but don't you think going to New York to spend Christmas with someone you've never even met is a little ..."

"Romantic?"

"I was going to say crazy."

Clementine waved away Paige's concern like an annoying fly. "Sam and I have poured our hearts out to each other for months now. What we have is real."

Sadie sighed, as only the jaded can, but she kept her mouth shut.

"What does Debra think?" Paige asked.

"She thinks I'm crazy too. We had a huge argument over it. She only backed down when I agreed to stay at a hotel and not at Sam's."

"She looks out for you."

"She's worse than my mother."

"At least someone is thinking straight," Paige said. "I know your generation do things differently, but still ..."

"I'm not a child, Paige."

"Darling, you're twenty-two, you're young, and this is so impulsive. Anything could happen. What if—"

"What if Sam is an axe murderer?" Clementine hooted with laughter. "That's what Debra said."

"Or a Republican," sniffed Sadie.

"Well, what if?" Paige said.

Clementine looked extremely young for a moment. "You know what I said to her?"

"What did you say?"

"I said, 'And what if Sam is the love of my life?'"

Eva

What we see depends mainly on what we look for.

John Lubbock

Christmas Eve

She'd made a mistake. Eva knew that now. She stared over the rim of the mug she was clutching and willed herself to stay calm.

Don't panic.

What had she been thinking, coming here alone? Around her, the Rathausplatz was crowded. The market laneways were packed and groups of people huddled together, laughing, drinking, and celebrating around the gluhwein stall. It was Christmas Eve in Vienna, and she did not belong here. Now if only her legs would move, then she could leave.

Instead she took a sip of her gluhwein.

And another. And prayed that the mulled wine would somehow sedate her. She tried to concentrate on what was happening externally, rather than internally. She could taste the cloves. An icy breeze nipped at the tip of her nose. With it came the strong smell of garlic from the langos stand. Her eyes darted around, taking in the scene. She was cold to her core, despite the hot mulled wine. Anxiety's freezing fingers were clutching at her. It was a fifteen-minute walk back to her hotel. Longer without legs that worked. She could hardly crawl. She felt foolish enough already without having to crawl down the Kärntner Strasse on Christmas Eve.

Take a deep breath. Four times.

Just like Paige had advised her to do, when she'd admitted she'd been feeling anxious lately.

What would Paige say now? *Focus on the scene around you, and not on yourself.*

Eva looked around her. Where was she?

She was at a gluhwein stand at the annual Magic of Advent in Vienna. The city hall loomed down over the scene like a watchful parent while the Rathausplatz came to life in its annual spellbinding Christmas celebration.

Look around. Don't focus on what you're feeling. What can you see?

The market was a wonderland. It reminded Eva of every picture-perfect Christmas card she'd ever received. She'd stopped by stalls filled with baskets of Christmas decorations. Each and every one seemed finely spun from some magical thread.

Stall after stall of sweets and pastries and pretzels and teas and soaps. She'd stuffed herself silly with the *gebrannte Mandeln* (toasted almonds) and *Maroni* (sweet chestnuts). Nearby was the truffle stall, where she'd paused earlier for what seemed like an eternity as she asked for one *Stück* of each: the *Milch Nougat Trüffel, Tiramisu Trüffel, Cappuccino Trüffel* and the *Eierlikör Trüffel.*

Excellent. Now what else?

Electric angels lined the sidewalks. The trees were lit up with candy canes and ornaments and waterfalls of light. There were some rides for children: a small train, a carousel and pony rides. There was a puppet show. A soft dusting of snow coated everything, enough to add to the overall effect but not yet turn to mud. And the whole scene was draped in lights.

Geoff would say it looked like a massive glow-worm had thrown up. She smiled at the thought. He was the first to admit, he was as romantic as a dose of strep throat.

Of course, that was the reason she was here.

Deep breath. What else?

In the middle of this spellbinding scene was the most beautiful Christmas tree Eva had ever laid eyes on. It was tall and alight with what looked like a swarm of fireflies. She felt like she was standing inside a snow globe she'd once owned as a child. She'd been obsessed with that snow globe. She'd shake it and stare into it, willing herself to suddenly be a part of that scene. And now she was.

But wishing to be a part of some enchanted scene when you're six was way better than being a part of it all at sixty. The market was everything she'd expected, and more. But at this moment, it was the last place on earth she wanted to be.

"You'd hate it," Geoff had said. "Christ, I can't think of anywhere I'd hate more."

She'd slipped her arms around him and snuggled into his chest. "Wouldn't you like to share a gluhwein with me in the snow?"

"You want gluhwein, I'll make you some here, at home. Think of it as gluhwein without the pneumonia."

"I don't want gluhwein at home. I want it in Vienna." She'd dreamed of visiting the Vienna Christmas markets for years. But Geoff had never been interested.

"You know I can't stand all that gross commercialism, Eva."

"But it's not like that. The first Christmas market was held in Vienna in 1296," she said, appealing to the historian in him. "It's a wonderful annual event steeped in tradition that goes back to the middle ages."

"Well, I'm more interested in my middle ages, and I hate the fucking cold."

"Darling, there's this tree, the Little Heart Tree, where lovers meet—"

"And freeze to death."

What was the point!

"You're so romantic."

And then he'd grab her, and pull her close, and his voice would growl. "I'd rather romance you somewhere hot."

"You mean you'd rather fuck me somewhere hot. Romance and fucking are different."

"Fucking is always hot with you."

And she'd catch a whiff of his scent, which never failed to make her dizzy. She'd try to talk him round, but he knew the effect he had on her. His hand would slip under her shirt, or slowly unbutton her pants. And all the while he'd challenge her, with his eyes, his slight smirk.

"You want flowers, or you want sex?" He knew the answer.

And each time he peeled off her clothes she knew she'd live a life without romance if she had to choose. In fact, she had. Because Geoff wouldn't give her both. And sex with Geoff was addictive and necessary. It was the glue that bound them, the one thing they always got right.

The last time she'd broached Christmas in Vienna he'd fucked her over the sofa, and then afterward, as she lay naked across it, trying to catch her breath, he walked over to his desk and sat down at the computer. He was naked, gloriously so. He was built like a gladiator. And as he booked their Christmas in Spain, he made sure he had the last word.

"This bloody dream of yours, better off keeping it as a dream. The reality of Christmas in Vienna will destroy it for you."

The bastard was right. Not because this wasn't beautiful, but because he wasn't with her. He never came, had never wanted to come with her, and coming alone was a huge mistake. It was a glaring reminder of every time he'd failed her, or refused her, or bulldozed over her to get his own way. Being here alone was a reminder of how she'd spent twenty years desperately wanting him to do something romantic for her, anything, anything. A bunch of flowers. A bloody poem. A loving dedication in one of his books. But she'd got nothing. If she dared mention it, he'd dig his heels in and challenge her to leave if she didn't like it. But she never left. Because she loved him. Totally and utterly.

So most of all … being in Vienna alone now was a reminder that he was dead.

Deep breath. Focus on something light. Something unrelated.

Eva stared at the children boarding the train. She tried to concentrate on them, what they were wearing, and their laughter. But she couldn't get her mind off Geoff.

Geoff had been dead a year. One year and ten days to be exact. While not officially her first Christmas without him, it was certainly the first she could remember. Last year didn't count. It was a blur. She'd been in a very dark place. She could barely remember his funeral, or the weeks afterward, where she couldn't get out of bed. She saw in the New Year clutching his shirt, wild with desire for a dead man, so grateful she'd been behind on the washing when he died. She had a bunch of his shirts that still smelled like him, but was petrified that the scent was fading.

There were moments during those first two months where she didn't think she'd survive. There were a few truly overwhelming moments when she prayed she wouldn't. But ultimately, Eva was not the type of woman to curl up and die alongside her man. One morning she got up and actually ate breakfast. She showered and then checked her emails. She sat alone, coffee in hand, by her favorite window where the morning sun flooded in. And she knew she'd be okay. She wanted to be okay. She was determined to rebuild her life.

It hadn't been easy. Thankfully she had her work. Editors like her were able to pick and choose. She escaped into the novels she edited. She escaped into the very world Geoff had always mocked—romance. Admittedly he didn't ridicule her work, or the romance writers they knew. Being a writer himself he was fully aware of how good writers bled for their art, irrespective of genre. For him, the problem was never about romance books, but that Eva expected that romance to translate into real life.

"That's like me suddenly becoming Henry VIII because I've just finished my book about him."

"Geoff, you are like him," Eva sniffed.

Working from home was both a blessing and a curse. Geoff was in every room, every piece of furniture. God knows he'd made the final decisions when they were renovating, so even if she preferred the beige hues, they ended up with bold colors. She liked the caramel-colored couch, but ended up with deep red. Now that he was gone, Eva took comfort in being surrounded by the remnants of his powerful personality.

Until she glimpsed his desk. And then she could feel herself slipping away, her skin and flesh and every atom of her being sliding off her into a pool on the floor. Being married to a writer meant he was at home and at his desk a lot. Unlike other women she knew, she couldn't kid herself that her husband was at the office late or on a business trip. His empty chair was a reminder. His absence was palpable and constant.

Eva had met Geoff later in life. They'd both been married, and divorced, with lots of baggage. She was on a romance panel at a historical writers' conference in Florida, and Geoff was the keynote speaker. She'd read a few of his novels, sprawling novels set in Tudor and Elizabethan England that were popular with both the literati and airport readers. She sat down the front of his session and watched him speak, mesmerized. He was one helluva man. Tall, dark hair, rugged, with muscular arms and an endless chest. And he knew how to work a crowd. He was articulate and erudite, but also had the audience in stitches. At one point, his eyes rested on her and her whole body filled with fire. Afterward, to her surprise, he came over to her and introduced himself.

"I find it unfair that you know my name and I don't yet know yours."

"I'm Eva." She shook his hand and a jolt of pure energy shot straight through her. She covered her surprise with nervous chat. "I enjoyed your talk. I absolutely agree with—"

Geoff cut her off, as was to become his habit in their relationship. "Fuck my talk. I'd rather have a drink with you."

Eva agreed to it without hesitation, another pattern in their relationship. Not that she was weak, then or ever. Quite the opposite. As she knew, from that very first night, only the strongest of women would take on a man like Geoff. Right from the start he was challenging, but Eva found it refreshing to be challenged. Every conversation was to the death. He kept her on her toes—and goddammit, she hadn't been off her heels in years till she met him.

He also kept her in bed. For three full days. By the final night of the conference, Eva was wondering how she'd live without him.

She ran her hand over his chest. It was everything a chest should be on a man. "I'm sure everyone at the conference is talking about us."

"Let them. It'll give them something to write about." Geoff moved a lock of hair from her face. "Want to stay here with me for Christmas?"

"In Florida?"

"In bed."

"But that's two weeks away?"

"So? You said your kids are with your ex this year. So are mine. And Christ knows I hate English weather at this time of year. Stay with me here." Geoff slipped his hand across her belly and down between her legs. "You're wet. I take that as a yes." He moved down and spread her legs, and slid his tongue inside her. Conversation over. But from that moment on, Christmas was about warm weather and lots of sex.

She never complained. Who would? Right when she'd thought it was all over for her, at thirty-nine, with a messy divorce and kids in tow … this ravishing man charged into her life and took over. He couldn't get enough of her. He didn't tell her she was beautiful or desirable, he showed her. He didn't have a romantic bone in his body. But he was passionate. From the moment he'd first kissed her on a Miami boardwalk, she was his. His smell, his build, the noises he made while he was inside her. There was no other man as male as Geoff. His very presence excited her. And ultimately subsumed her. And that never changed in twenty years. Not until the day she found him dead on the floor from a heart attack. His heart. The one organ he gave on his terms.

'Entschuldigen Sie, bitte, ist der Tisch frei?'

Eva plummeted back to the present. A young man was standing in front of her.

"I'm sorry, I don't speak German."

"I was just asking if this table is free. Are you waiting on friends?"

"No, please go ahead." She gestured at the vacant area around her table, and the young man and his friend moved in and started talking.

She watched them for a moment and then turned her attention elsewhere. Perhaps she should've brought someone to Vienna with her. But who?

Eva was in touch with all the kids—her own and Geoff's—and pretended for their sakes that she was managing okay. She lied, and said she was getting out and seeing people. But she wasn't. Their circle of friends was very much a couples affair. And she still wasn't up to socializing without Geoff. Not with their old friends.

She had Paige now, of course. Their friendship was new but already ran deep. In fact, in many ways it had saved her.

After the initial grief had abated and she was able to work again, Eva spent her days editing. Then, in the afternoon, she'd go for a walk, often stopping by her local bookstore. She'd always supported her local bookstore, but after Geoff's death she found herself haunting the aisles of the cozy little shop more than ever before. She went in to look at Geoff's books, despite having shelves of them at home. She'd pick up his books, stare at his photo on the jacket, and flick through to the dedication: *To my sidekick, Eva.*

Sidekick.

Never love. Or darling. Or wife.

He'd published three novels while they were together before she confronted him about his choice of endearment.

"Why don't you say, 'To my wife'? Or my darling?"

"Why don't I wear yellow? It's just not me."

"Aren't I your darling?"

"Right now you're my pain in the arse."

And he'd given her a kiss and returned to his work. It was another novel, and when he published it, he dedicated it to his sidekick.

That was Geoff. And she knew that. But still, she was drawn over and over into that shop to open the books, as if by some miracle he'd posthumously change the wording and be romantic.

It was on one of those afternoons that she noticed Paige peering over her shoulder.

"Is that you? The sidekick?" Paige asked.

Eva nodded.

"I'm so sorry for your loss. He was a great writer."

"Yes, he was."

Paige tilted her head to one side. "He talked about you a lot."

Eva stared at the woman. "Did you know him?"

"He did a reading here once."

"Oh, that's right."

"And he'd sometimes pop in and buy something. Whenever he did, he'd point out all the books his wife edited."

"All my romance books?"

Paige nodded. "He was very proud of you."

Much to her own horror, Eva burst into tears. "Why couldn't he acknowledge that, rather than calling me his bloody sidekick?"

"I know, darling. Men can be such bastards."

And from that moment on they were friends. Paige told Eva about the book club she ran, so she had joined. It was the darkest time in her life, and the friendship and support she'd received from this group of women had been such a blessing. They'd read books: always inspiring, uplifting tales, romances and biographies about great women. Just the type of read Eva loved and needed. Looking back, the one thing that had saved her from complete despair was her book club, and the women she'd befriended.

Book by book, month by month, meeting by meeting, Eva felt the weight of her grief lift. Not disappear, mind you, but it was unlikely that would ever happen. She didn't know if she'd want it to. A man like Geoff would be mourned forever. She knew that was the risk she was taking the moment she met him.

It was Paige who had encouraged her to spend Christmas in Vienna. She'd been insistent, even when they'd spoken today, when for once Paige needed Eva's support.

"It's about closure, Eva."

"It's just bad timing," Eva said down the phone.

"No, it's perfect timing. I need your support next week. So please go and do this. It's part of your grieving process, Eva." Paige gave her a hug. "You'll be more use to me afterward."

Eva knew Paige was right.

Paige pointed out. "And you've always wanted to go.

"I always wanted to go with him," Eva said. "But no, we always went somewhere hot."

"Yes, how dreadful for you," Paige teased. "Morocco and rampant sex for Christmas. I do think you were a little blind to what you did have. I was lucky if Tim ever gave me a card."

Eva laughed. "You always know how to cheer me up."

"And you always know how to depress me," Paige said with a wink. "Remember, I met your husband. He was gorgeous."

"God, I know. But not a romantic bone in his body."

"Perhaps. But my husband was spineless, and believe me, that's worse."

Eva blinked as snowflakes landed on her eyelashes. She knew Paige was right, but still couldn't help feeling angry with him right now. All she'd wanted was a little romance. She'd wanted him to bring her to Vienna. She wanted to kiss him under the Viennese Little Heart Tree. She'd dreamed about kissing someone she loved beneath its branches ever since she'd first read about that goddamn tree. It was the place for lovers to meet in Vienna.

Too late now.

She began to calm. The anxiety passed. The breathing helped. Or perhaps it was the gluhwein. She finished it and placed the mug on the table. She would now make her way back to the hotel and try to find an early flight home.

She took one last look around. Eva noticed a small striped tent off to one side. The cloth across the entrance was pulled back and she could see a woman seated at a small table, watching her. She glanced at the sign outside: *Wahrsagerin. Bitte kommen Sie rein.* A psychic?

She looked back at the woman, who motioned for her to enter.

Oh, what the hell!

This was one of the benefits of not having Geoff with her. He would make some derisive comment and hurry her past the tent. But Eva had always been interested in psychic phenomena. And she'd be lying if she weren't just the slightest bit curious. Would she ever be able to move on from Geoff? Perhaps this woman would know the answer to that.

Eva entered the tent and the woman waved her into a seat. Neither of them spoke. Instead, the woman seemed to wait for Eva to get her bearings. The tent was warm, with a soft glow and the smell of roses. The table was draped in a purple velvet cloth and on it sat a pack of tarot cards and a crystal ball. Eva almost laughed. This psychic certainly had the tools. And the look. Eva guessed she was Romany, probably in her forties, with incredible dark eyes that seemed to stare straight through her. She had on the expected outfit, big skirt, lots of jewelry, a colorful scarf wrapped around her luscious black hair. When she spoke, her English was excellent, with a lyrical accent.

"You are okay now?"

Eva was thrown. Had the woman been watching her fighting off her panic attack?

"How do you know I speak English?"

The gypsy sat motionless. "How do I know anything? I just know."

Never wiser words spoken, thought Eva.

The woman stuck out her palm. Eva placed her own hand on top and was then embarrassed when the psychic sniffed and said, "Payment, please."

"Oh, I'm sorry. I thought … just a moment." Eva dug into her bag and found her wallet. She remembered she'd spent all her change. "I don't have gold … to cross your palm or whatever …"

The psychic shrugged. "I take Visa too."

Eva hid her surprise by burrowing through her bag and finding her emergency stash. "It's okay, I have enough euro."

The woman clutched the notes and shoved them under the table, storing them god knows where. Eva certainly wasn't going to ask. Then she turned her attention back to Eva.

"You are very sad."

Eva nodded. You didn't need to be psychic to see that. Her friend's granddaughter had recently said the same thing to her, and she was six.

"Your heart is broken."

Eva hated that she was so cynical but that ole chestnut was pretty much a sure thing in a psychic reader's tent. Women didn't enter here because they were happy.

"He is sorry he was not more … romantic."

All the air in the tent was suddenly sucked out.

Eva reeled back as though she'd been slapped. "What did you say?"

"He is sorry. He says … I don't understand this, but he tells me … sidekick."

Eva held the side of the table, bunching the velvet cloth in her hands. "Is he here?"

The psychic shook her head and Eva took a breath, suddenly relieved. Of course he wasn't here. How ridiculous.

109

"He is outside. He doesn't like my tent." The gypsy smiled at Eva. "He's a big man. Perhaps his ego would not fit in here." She let out a husky laugh. "He says you were right, it's nice here. But bloody cold."

Eva stared at her in horror. She felt faint.

How can she know all that? Because she's a professional con artist! The woman must be a fraud.

She was feeding on her need, her grief. But how would she know Geoff wasn't romantic?

Because that's a common failing in men?

How would she know about being his sidekick?

Eva had no comeback for that.

The woman leaned across the table. "He says he is sorry. He is here now."

A sob caught in Eva's throat. She'd heard enough.

"That's enough. Thank you for your time." Eva grabbed her bag and hastily made her way out of the tent. The night air hit her like a slap, back to reality.

Stupid, stupid, stupid. Those gypsy women feed on people like me.

That thought made her feel better. She would hardly be the first woman in history to waste money on a charlatan.

She began to walk, her hands thrust deep into her coat pockets. She headed back toward the city hall. She'd catch the U-Bahn back to Karlsplatz and her hotel. She'd planned to walk, but Vienna at night held no appeal anymore. She felt better now she'd made her decision to leave. It wasn't the right time, or the right place for her.

Out of the corner of her eye she noticed a couple kissing under the Little Heart Tree, off to her left. A tear escaped and trickled down her cheek. She was suddenly enraged. She felt like shaking them. How dare they flaunt their love like that. And did they understand how precious it was? Probably not. She hadn't appreciated how little time she'd have with Geoff.

And now he was gone, and life was hard, so very hard. And she'd just made it worse by going into that tent.

She grabbed a tissue from her pocket and dabbed her eyes. She was allowed to grieve, for as long as she needed to. And she wanted to do that at home, where she felt closer to him. Not here, in the last place on earth he'd ever be.

"Eva."

It was like a short sharp shout that echoed in her head. She turned. Did she know someone here? Surely not. And how embarrassing to run into someone from home, when her eyes were all red.

She looked around, but didn't see anyone she knew.

Now I'm hearing things.

And at that moment the young couple under the Little Heart Tree finished going for gold and stepped away, and she saw him, right there where they'd been kissing. She knew it couldn't be him. It shouldn't be him. But it was. Leaning against the tree was Geoff, watching her.

She blinked a few times, but he was there. She didn't move. She couldn't. She was absolutely frozen. She waited for him to do something, anything. But he didn't. He just stared at her … and she stared back. She wanted to run to him, to touch him, to hold him close and never again let go … but she didn't dare move because she somehow understood the absolute fragility of this moment. One final moment …

And then the world re-entered.

"Entschuldigen!" a man's voice apologized as he jostled her to one side. She staggered, and when she looked up again, Geoff was gone.

She pushed her way through the crowd, to the tree. Where was he?

"Geoff. Geoff!"

Another couple stepped out of her way and gave her a strange look as she passed.

"GEOFF!"

Eva circled the tree. Nothing. She paused in the spot where he'd been standing. Gone. A sob escaped her throat. Her hand flew of its own accord to her chest. Oh god, he'd been there. He'd been there for her. She lifted her chin upward, looking through the branches of the Little Heart Tree at the sky beyond. Snowflakes fell on her face. She'd never got her kiss here. But he'd come. He was here for here. And it was enough.

Clementine

Clem,

This is your Christmas present. It's a keychain stun gun that lets off five million volts. Now listen carefully. DO NOT CARRY THIS ON THE PLANE. Pack it in your suitcase. Then, when you get to New York, carry it on you at all times. Not because New York is dangerous. It's not. It's a great city. But if Sam is a psychopathic axe murderer, then you have this to protect you.

Love,

Deb

PS: Make sure you go to the Met, and the carousel at Central Park and also Times Square. Don't bother with the Empire State Building. You don't like heights and there's heavy security. They might question the stun gun.

*

Dear Debra,

Thank you!!!!! You always give me the best pressies.

Where are you? You haven't answered my texts. Your phone is off. You're not in your room. You're never up this early, which means you didn't come home last night. Can you let me know you're okay?

Anyway, by the time you read this, I'll be on my way to New York. I took your advice. I'm staying at the Montana Hotel on Lexington Ave. And I'll be carrying your Christmas present, so even if Sam is a psychopathic axe murderer, I'm safe.

I know you think I'm nuts, but you don't know Sam like I do.

Please support me. Don't be angry with me. I can't stand not talking to you. I miss hanging out with you all the time. I miss my best friend. I want to share this with you. I'm so excited. Sam thinks I'm going to Spain after all—what a surprise when I knock on the door!!!!!

I'll be back on New Year's Eve. I'd love to see the New Year in with you. Please, please, please. Stop being such a moody cow and call me.

Love you,
Clem

Amanda

Could a greater miracle take place than for us to look through each other's eyes for an instant?

Henry David Thoreau

Christmas Day

Amanda hated that she was nervous. Wasn't Christmas meant to be relaxing? Perhaps it was for some people … Like, Dylan, her son. But then a constant diet of Minecraft and A-grade weed (of course she knew!) was bound to help numb his brain. Granted, Dylan's twin, Caitlin, wasn't very relaxed, but Amanda suspected that was because she'd recently gone on the pill (either that or she'd had breast implants) and it was affecting her hormones (even more than being sixteen did). Usually psychotic in spurts, Caitlin had turned into Medusa twenty-four hours a day. Amanda could hear her now, screaming at Zack, who, in true ten-year-old style, added fuel to the fire by mimicking her.

Amanda was tempted to drop a Valium, but the last time she'd done that was three years ago when Peter's parents came for Christmas lunch. They'd left that day finally understanding why Peter had dumped Amanda for Maxine. Maxine would never fall asleep on the turkey.

Not that it mattered now. Maxine and her immaculate manners were history. As were Charlotte, and Martina, and Kat. Peter went through women like Amanda went through Kleenex in spring. His behavior was also due to allergies. Peter was allergic to commitment.

Until now.

Peter had been with Alice for six months and the changes were obvious. He wasn't as brash, or as loud, or as annoying anymore. He didn't need to be the center of attention constantly. He was present and focused when he was with the kids, and he rarely glanced at his watch during the prerequisite swap-over conversation he had with Amanda.

Amanda had always managed to maintain a semblance of friendliness with Peter, for the sake of the children, but she still disliked the bastard. Not because he'd left her for Maxine. Oh no, she'd disliked Peter for years before he'd finally walked. Year by year as their marriage unraveled she had marveled at the fact that she'd bred with someone so completely self-absorbed. She would often stare at him across the dinner table and wonder what it was that had brought them together. What she'd fallen for. It was as though she had relationship amnesia.

If she'd found it difficult to put her finger on then, it was impossible now. He was a stranger. A stranger she saw in her children—and if she was honest, it annoyed her a lot. She hated it when Zack's lips curled at a certain angle just before he yelled, and when Dylan gave her a patronizing snarl, and there was this thing that Caitlin did with her chin—pure Peter! And in those moments she'd try so hard to find even a dying ember of that thing she'd loved in Peter, so much that they'd had these kids.

But recently, he'd changed. He'd been, if not completely likable, then close to it. Their conversations were pleasant. While there had certainly been times when she'd fantasized about Peter being hit by a comet, the truth was she'd fantasized more often about him treating her with respect. Peter's recent behavior gave Amanda hope that they were headed in that direction. And it was during one of their more enjoyable conversations that Zack had asked if his father could come over for Christmas and Amanda had agreed. Bring Alice, she'd said at the time. It would be good for the kids.

Amanda had never met Alice, which was why she was now nervous.

"Maaaaaaarm."

It was never just Mum. It was always a dragged-out, neighborhood cats brawling, caterwauling, fingernails on a blackboard sound that emanated from Caitlin's mouth. Amanda often tried to recall those distant days when she'd bounced her daughter on her lap and encouraged her to say, "Mum, mum, mum." It was the sweetest sound in the world back then and she was riddled with guilt that it bugged her so much now.

"What, Caitlin?"

Caitlin marched into the kitchen. "Zack just told me to eff off."

Amanda glanced at the top cupboard that housed the Valium. It was calling her name in a much sweeter voice than any of her children had used for years.

"Caity … please, just do me a favor and ignore him. He's ten … and male …"

No other explanation needed. Even Caitlin nodded. She turned to leave but Amanda stopped her.

"Caity … are you and Damien having sex?"

Caitlin looked as though Amanda had just asked her to eat a live kitten sandwich.

"I was young once too, you know." Amanda blanched, horrified by her own inanity. She changed tack. "I adore babies, but I don't want to be a grandmother just yet."

"You won't be."

"Seriously, darling, I couldn't handle it. I'm only forty-two. I'd go nuts if you got pregnant."

"I won't."

"But accidents happen."

"Mum, I'm on the pill …"

Ka-ching! She'd walked straight into that one. Amanda patted her daughter's arm and moved over to the sink, where the turkey was laying stark naked, legs in the air. Amanda sighed. Apparently she was the only one in the room who never found herself in that position.

"Anything else you want to know?" Caitlin's voice was a mixture of fear and loathing.

"Yeah, sure, what's Alice like?"

Caitlin stared at the ceiling for a moment, as though the answer was hanging from it. "She's cool."

That was a given. All Peter's girlfriends had been cool. It came with the territory. He'd dated a trail of young, success-ful hipsters, who fed his ego and drained his bank account. Amanda hardly considered herself to be a complete nanna. She'd been one of London's hottest stylists when she'd met Peter. Back then, she too was thin and gorgeous, a regular on the scene … She'd boinked Michael Hutchence in a nightclub toilet once, for christsake.

That version of her was as dead as her celebrity shag.

Nowadays, her hips were bigger, her breasts were smaller, and no amount of make-up could hide the lines around her eyes, but she didn't feel completely unattractive. And she had a wardrobe most women would kill for, thanks to her boutique, the Pantry. (Her boutique that Peter had often called her hobby, but was in fact one of the things she was most proud of.) She knew she wasn't ready for the wreckers just yet. It's just there were moments, usually moments when she was feeling good about herself, that she would catch a glimpse in the mirror ... and she looked like her mother. Amanda had morphed into her mum, and that was never a good thing for a woman's self-esteem. Especially when the women Peter now dated were so young.

She could picture Alice now, sexy, edgy and streamlined—a bit like Peter's new Mercedes—and it made her want to puke. Instead, she grabbed a handful of stuffing and shoved it up the turkey's arse.

"Oh, turkey, I christen thee Peter ..."

The phone rang, but before she could pull her hand out of Peter the turkey's arse, Zack pounced on it.

"Who is it, Zack?"

Amanda could hear Zack having one of his one-ear-on-the-TV-the-other-on-the-phone conversations. "Yeah ... yeah ... yeah ... I'll tell her."

Zack hung up and returned to the television.

"Tell me what?" Amanda called out.

"Something about Dad's brother being here for lunch."

"He doesn't have a brother."

"Oh, and they're running late."

"Your father? Late?"

Amanda yanked her hand out of the turkey and a big chunk of stuffing flew through the air and hit her in the head.

"Oh for f ... udge fudge fuck."

Amanda washed her hands in the sink and then ran her fingers across her hair. Yep, just as she'd suspected. Stuffing in her hair. Lucky they were late. It had to be Alice's fault, because Peter was a stickler for being on time. If she and the kids weren't ready to walk out the door ten minutes before they needed to, all hell would break loose. Dylan had christened his father "The Minute Nazi."

Amanda zipped into the bathroom, hung her head over the sink and washed the stuffing from her hair, which ruined the blow-dry she'd paid for yesterday afternoon. She raised her head and looked in the mirror and willed herself not to cry.

"It's only hair."

It wasn't only hair. It was her pride. It was her shield today, against her failed marriage and Peter's new-found happiness. Against her single status. She wanted Peter's girlfriend to see that she too could have a boyfriend if she wanted. That she hadn't been tossed aside. That she was freaking fabulous too. But now she had naff hair, which clearly indicated she was anything but.

"Why do I care what she thinks?" Amanda muttered.

She combed her hair down. It was a lost cause now. At least she had a great cut and color. There was no sign of the dark roots or stray gray. Not on her head anyway. She'd recently found her first gray *down there*. She was mortified. How would she ever let any man near it again? She'd shared the news with Sadie, her friend from her book club, who also happened to be the most interesting person she'd met in years. Her advice was to get a Brazilian.

"Seriously, I can't believe you still have a jungle down there. I know it's kind of retro and cool right now, but honey, if it's going gray, get rid of it."

Amanda had nearly peed her pants laughing, as she often did when she was with Sadie. But there was no way she was waxing *that*. As far as she was concerned, bald ones were *not* for adult women.

Amanda checked the house for the tenth time. Reasonably clean, reasonably tidy, with an air of faux cheer thanks to the overdecorated tree. She'd long since removed any obvious signs of Peter, apart from some photos in the kids' rooms. Alice wouldn't know that they'd bought the piano on a whim, thinking it would be fun to learn to play together. (They never did.) Alice would see the couch and form an opinion on its shape and color, but not know that Zack had been conceived there. Amanda drifted over to the tree. Alice might notice all the decorations, but how could she know that each and every ornament had been bought somewhere different, on one of their trips overseas. The Christkindlmarkt in Vienna, the Marché Saint-Germain in Paris ... Bergdorf Goodman in New York. And perched on the top was the star Peter had bought her in Venice and placed on the tree himself each and every year of their marriage. For the past three years, Amanda had clambered up there and done it herself with the help of a stool and a strong vodka cranberry juice.

Peter was lucky. He'd walked out this door and straight into his brand-spanking-new apartment where there were no ghosts to haunt him. It would be easy to shag someone new in a new apartment. Even if Amanda did finally meet someone, she could hardly shag on the kitchen floor. She still remembered Peter puking there. (Dodgy oyster ... nearly killed him.) Or in the shower with the tiles she hated, but that Peter had insisted on.

Peter still lived here, embedded in the walls, whether she liked it or not. Perhaps it was time to move. She'd moved on, emotionally. That wasn't the problem. She didn't want him back. She wasn't angry with him anymore. Not constantly, anyway. And she definitely dreamed of meeting someone else. She'd been on a few dates, no one special, but she was certainly open to loving again. More than that, she yearned for it. But where the hell would she meet a man? She ran the Pantry and was a full-time taxidriver/tutor/shrink/jailer for the kids. Ideally, the perfect man would just ring the doorbell. Today would be nice. Santa's perfect delivery—FedSex. Like that would ever happen.

If Peter got her anything for Christmas she'd probably die of shock. She'd spent every year of their marriage hoping, praying he'd get her something decent for Christmas. It never happened. The first few years he got her underwear: the type of lacy lingerie that men buy women thinking they're being generous, when everyone knows the gift is for them. Around their fourth Christmas together, Peter had started giving her whitegoods and household appliances. The vacuum for the car was a particularly memorable year.

Peter hadn't bothered getting Amanda anything since the divorce. She at least made the effort and got the kids a gift to give him. Admittedly last year it was an aftershave she knew he hated. But this year, with his girlfriend in tow, there was no way she was going to look like the bitter ex-wife. She'd bought them a gourmet hamper from Fortnum & Mason.

Amanda relaxed a little. The house looked fine. It would all be okay. She just needed to … stop sweating. *What?* Why was she sweating?

"DYLAN!!!!" Amanda legged it down the hall and flung open his bedroom door. "Did you turn the heating up again?"

"Did you knock?"

"I'll knock you. I've told you not to do that."

"I'm cold."

"Because you haven't moved for a week. Get up, get the blood flowing."

She was about to lecture him on drugs, blood clots and teenage mental illness when the doorbell rang.

"Goddammit, Dylan." Like it was his fault.

The doorbell was Amanda's cue to *really* start sweating. Not moist palms and a light sheen. More like "I've just run a marathon across the Sahara Desert" type sweat.

"Turn that bloody heater down now!" she snapped and bolted for her room.

She grabbed the handtowel in her bathroom and pressed it under her armpits. Then she lifted her arm and took a sniff. Not good.

The doorbell rang again and she heard Zack bounding down the hall. Being ten, he hadn't yet reached the Age of Lethargy.

Amanda gave herself a quick wash, a coat of deodorant, a dab of scented oil, and slipped on a fresh shirt. It wasn't new, like the other one, but at least it didn't smell like a camel. She glanced in the mirror, saw her mother ... and wished to hell she kept the Valium in the bathroom instead of the kitchen.

"Maaaaaaaaaaaaaaaarrrrrrrrm!!!!!!"

Time to face them. Christ she hated Christmas.

Amanda made her way down the hall. She could hear Peter talking, and then laughter ... Dylan's, Zack's, Caitlin's ... and another laugh, husky, sexy ... Alice.

Amanda flapped her arms up and down to ward off more sweat. She felt like the turkey ... and just as helpless. Three deep breaths and a couple more flaps ... and she marched straight into battle.

"Sorry, everyone, I just had to ..." Amanda locked eyes with Alice. The whole room spun like a roulette wheel: place your bets. It couldn't be ...

Alice looked just as stunned. She moved toward Amanda.

And suddenly both woman burst into tears. Peter started to introduce them, but they didn't seem to hear him.

"Mandy?"

"Ali?"

They flew into each other's arms.

"Oh my god! Ali! Is it you? It's you?"

"It's me. Mandy ... I never ... I just ... Oh, wow, Amanda?" Alice touched Amanda's face, as if she wasn't sure she was real.

Amanda's tears flowed. "I can't believe it."

And they held each other tight again.

"I know, I know."

Alice and Amanda finally withdrew from their embrace and stood facing each other. Peter and the kids stared at them, speechless, countless questions hanging thick in the air. There was a moment of absolute silence. And then Amanda's tears turned to laughter.

"Holy crap, this is a coincidence!"

*

Amanda and Alice sat under the shade of the Brighton Pier, each with a bag of sweets they were too upset to eat.

"I can't believe she's marrying him," Alice said.

"I think we're meant to be happy for her, Ali." Amanda looked anything but. "He's nice. It's not like you're going to get the stepdad from hell."

"He's not that nice if he expects us to move." Alice pushed her toes through the sand. "I'll never find another friend like you."

"I hope not. I couldn't bear it if you replaced me."

Amanda wrapped her arms around her best friend and both of them started to cry with the despair only sixteen-year-old girls can feel.

"Promise you'll write every week, Mandy."

"I promise." Amanda grabbed Ali's arms and forced her friend to look at her. "And we'll never lose touch. Ever."

"Never," Alice cried. "I promise."

Amanda scrambled up and scurried around the beach. She found an open scallop shell and snapped it in half. She handed one half to Alice.

"I call upon the power of the ocean to hear our request."

Alice jumped up, eager to join in.

Amanda continued. "We, Mandy and Ali, are like this shell. If the waves wash us away from each other, we ask that they also bring us back together."

"*However that may be,*" whispered Alice.

And with that both girls threw their half of the shell into the sea.

*

"So you went to school together?" Peter was still trying to piece the story together.

"For two and a half years. We were joined at the hip that whole time," Alice explained. "Then my mother remarried and we moved again."

"We stayed in touch for a while, but eventually lost track of each other." Amanda was still shaking her head in disbelief. "Why was that?"

"I don't know. We moved a few times within a year. Things weren't great. Mum's marriage didn't work out. I kept writing, though."

"We moved too. Dad was promoted and we came to London," Amanda explained. "I remember calling your number to tell you, but it was disconnected. I was devastated. I tried writing, but there was no reply. I cried for months."

"I never got your letter."

"I searched for you online when we first got internet, but there were so many Ali Mathesons out there."

"I took my stepdad's name in the end, so I became Alice Gottman. But I searched for you too."

Amanda held her hands out in a "me too" type gesture. "Pete and I married quite young, and I was so glad to get rid of the surname Bangs, I took his on."

Amanda and Alice sang in unison, "Amanda Bangs ... oh no she don't!" And then they both howled with laughter, until Amanda noticed how ill at ease Peter looked.

"The fates were against us," Amanda said.

"Until now."

Amanda was in shock, although the strong vodka lime she'd made was helping. Peter's Alice was her Alice. The most intense friendship she'd ever had. She didn't know what was more surprising: that Peter was shagging her childhood friend, or that he was shagging someone like Alice. Alice Matheson was not Peter's type. And surely she hadn't changed that much. She certainly looked the same.

Alice wasn't a pretty young hipster. She was all blonde wisps and soft curves. Amanda had initially taken her under her wing at school out of pity, but from that sprang a very real friendship. Alice was bookish, a bit clumsy, could sing, and had a birthmark on her stomach that she hated. Looking at her now, Alice still looked clumsy, and bookish. She was pretty, but age had faded the ethereal quality she once had and added a couple of pounds. Now she simply looked attractive, in a somewhat inconspicuous way.

One by one the kids drifted off to their rooms, leaving the adults to piece together the happenstance. The questions flowed as fast as the vodka. Amanda realized that she'd never asked any questions about Alice out of self-preservation.

"Where did you two meet?"

Alice glanced at Peter.

Jesus bloody hell, she really loves him! Amanda took a large swig of necessity.

"Peter's firm handled my divorce."

Amanda pursed her lips and Peter frowned at her.

"It wasn't my case, Amanda. I met Alice in the lift."

"I'm not judging, Peter." Amanda turned back to Alice. "So you're just divorced."

"Yes, but separated for a few years. Nothing new."

"Kids?"

Alice's face fell. "No. I can't."

Alice wanted to reach out and offer comfort, but the years apart had stripped her of the ability to do that. "That must be difficult."

"FUCK OFF, ZACK!" Caitlin's bellows echoed through the house.

All three adults paused for a moment, and then Alice broke the tension with, "Difficult? Only sometimes."

Amanda smiled gratefully. "I thought the teenage years were tough when I was a teen … but this is unbearable."

It didn't seem to faze Alice. "It's normal. And it's better that she's strong-willed, rather than a pushover."

True. "So what do you do?"

"I'm a pediatrician."

Amanda clapped her hands together. "Oh, you always wanted to be!" And then without thinking, she blurted, "At what age can doctors prescribe the pill without parental consent?"

Peter almost fell off his chair. "Are you talking about Caitlin?"

"No, I'm talking about Zack. Who do you think?"

"Is she having sex?"

"Well, you don't take the pill to go barn dancing, Peter."

Peter looked like he was about to implode, but then Alice placed her hand on his leg and gently pointed out, "At least she's being responsible, Pete."

Peter nodded and Amanda could almost hear the fizzle as his black mood passed. She was impressed. No one had ever stopped one of Peter's tantrums in its tracks before.

Peter turned back to Amanda and scowled. "It's always bloody Caitlin. Never the boys."

"Perhaps the reason Dylan hasn't had sex yet is because he's always too stoned."

A wave of anguish engulfed Peter's features. The intensity of it surprised Amanda and she suddenly understood that

Peter not only knew about Dylan, but was also consumed with worry.

"Why are you bringing all this up now, Amanda?" he asked.

Why indeed? She looked at Alice, a complete stranger, yet still so familiar. Amanda poured herself another drink. Was she already drunk? If not now, she soon would be. Alice held out her own glass as well.

"You're right, Peter," Amanda admitted. "Inappropriate timing. I've refrained from telling you all this, hoping you'd notice yourself. And you have. I underestimated you. Sorry." Amanda pulled herself together. "I also kept it to myself because I didn't want your new girlfriend to know my problems, but now that I know it's Alice … perhaps I'm just letting loose."

"You're in shock," Alice said. "I know I am. And I'm not sure how to deal with this. I always wanted to find you, Mandy. I figured we'd meet again, somewhere. But never in my wildest dreams …"

All three were quiet for a moment.

"Where do we go from here?" Amanda realized she was asking them both. She watched as Alice turned to Peter, as though he knew the answer. Amanda recoiled slightly at the look in Alice's eyes. Love. Pure love. Aimed at Peter. And it was in that instant that something shifted for Amanda. A veil lifted and she gazed at Peter and saw him through Alice's eyes.

Peter noticed her looking at him and smiled. It was the first genuinely loving smile she'd seen aimed her way in years. It completely floored her. She'd forgotten *that* smile, and when she saw it, the floodgates opened and a million memories came pouring out. Their first heady days of dating, the day they signed the papers for their first apartment, as he got down on one knee to propose, as he watched her walk down the aisle toward him, as he leaned over her encouraging her to push and then later when she handed Dylan to him. So many good memories. Where had they been hidden?

Amanda blinked back tears. She looked at Peter, but she wasn't imagining things. The smile was still there. And more. A glimmer of fun.

"I think we should all get drunk," he said. "And just talk. It'll be okay. There must be a reason for this."

So that's exactly what they did. The turkey burned, so the kids ate cake. The vodka ran out, so they popped open the champagne. Amanda couldn't deny that the connection was still there with Alice. They laughed and talked and even shed a couple of tears. But mostly Peter made them laugh. Amanda had forgotten how funny he was. How he'd made her laugh so hard in their early days together—that had been why she'd fallen for him, despite the fact that they weren't that compatible otherwise.

Unlike Peter and Alice. Amanda had to admit that they seemed to belong together. They fit: hand in glove. There was an easy rhythm, an unspoken language, stolen glances that conveyed an infinite conversation. She'd never had that with Peter. They'd loved each other, once. But they were never truly compatible. She'd only ever had that once, years before she'd met Peter. Once … with her first love.

"You know, there's one subject I've been avoiding, Alice … but I'm drunk enough to put it out there now." Amanda hiccupped slightly to confirm that fact. "How is your brother?"

*

Amanda and Tom clutched each other like he was going off to war.

"It's okay, Mandy. I'll see you again. I'm moving to York, not Mars."

"It feels like Mars." She wiped her tears on his shirt. "I love you."

"I love you too."

Tom started peeling Amanda off him, and Alice stepped into the gap. "One last hug."

The two girls sobbed, until Tom took his sister by the arm and helped her into the car, where his mother was patiently waiting.

Amanda stood on the curb as the car pulled out, and then crying, she chased it down the road, both Alice and Tom waving at her from the rear window.

And then they were gone.

*

"You know Tom?" Peter asked.

"Know him?" Amanda let out a loud laugh. "Peter ... I lost my virginity to him. Oh lord, he was the hottest guy at school. My first real boyfriend. I loved him. The three of us were inseparable. I was absolutely heartbroken when he left. When they both left."

Peter glanced at Alice then back at Amanda. "Did Zack give you my message?"

Amanda brushed Peter off. "Yes, Peter, he told me you'd be late." *Now back to Alice and more important things*, she thought. "Where does Tom live?"

"He just moved back to London from Munich ...' Alice said. 'He's divorced, so he's alone for the holidays and ...'

Peter tried to interrupt again. "I hope you don't mind, but I thought—"

The doorbell cut him off. Amanda clambered unsteadily to her feet.

"Hold that thought. Probably one of the neighbors."

"But Amanda, I forgot to tell you that—"

Amanda was sashaying toward the entrance, champagne glass still in hand. "Wait a minute, Peter. Let me just get this first."

Peter and Alice exchanged a look. They jumped to their feet and ran after her, just in time to see Amanda open the door.

To Tom.

Tall, broad shouldered, and drop-dead handsome! She would have recognized him anywhere. It was all still there. The sexy smile, the endless lashes, the stare that had defined her teen years. Tom, her Tom, was on her doorstep, holding a bottle of vintage Krug and looking just as stunned as she felt.

A thousand images flashed between them: lazy days at the beach, illicit Bacardis, strains of Dire Straits and Tears for Fears and Spandau Ballet. The first night they made love ... and the countless times after. Tom had been the first man to kiss Amanda all over. Amanda blinked, but nothing changed: he was still there, a little older, a little gray, and looking very confused. And then he smiled and it was like someone had finally let the sun back into her world.

"Look what Santa brought me." Amanda began to laugh.

Peter approached nervously. "I tried to tell you, Amanda. I asked Tom to drop by. Hope you don't mind."

"Mind?" Amanda wrapped her arms around her ex-husband and held him for the first time in years. "Peter, it's the best Christmas you've ever given me."

Clementine

Christmas Eve

Clementine caught a cab from JFK into the city, which she absolutely could not afford, especially in midday traffic. But now that she'd arrived, her bravado had disappeared. New York suddenly seemed very alien and rather scary. She did mental math all the way to the hotel, first converting her pounds to dollars and then working out the dent the cab ride put in her spending money.

Fortunately her parents had agreed to pay for the hotel. They weren't thrilled about her traipsing off to America to be with someone she'd met online. But Clementine assured them that she'd be in touch regularly, and was old enough to make these decisions herself.

She still let them pay for the hotel, though.

As it turned out, the hotel was very nice. Nothing too fancy, but certainly not one of those dodgy, dark hotels that she saw in some movies. She'd been imagining having to put a chair against her door, and finding syringes in her bed. But the Montana was a seven-story building in a lovely-looking area.

The foyer was bright and neat, and she was greeted by a very polite man in a smart suit and tie.

"You've booked a double. Will it just be you staying with us?"

"My partner might be joining me, but I don't know yet." She didn't know if Sam's roommate was around. If so, they could come here for some privacy.

He tapped on the computer for a moment and then smiled, the epitome of charm. "Not a problem. Just let us know so room service can arrange more towels."

"Great. Thanks."

He handed her the room key. "There's a special Christmas buffet in the breakfast room tomorrow, on the house."

Clementine *loved* a good buffet. "Awesome. Thanks."

She made her way to the lift. Fortunately the hotel wasn't fancy enough for a porter. Clementine had been nervous for days about how much to tip. Her room was simple and small but nice. She felt much more secure once she was in it and had locked the door. She was suddenly very grateful for Debra. As annoyed as she'd been at the time, having this room was the right thing to do. She was already nervous about surprising Sam. She couldn't imagine just rocking up there without coming here first to prepare.

And to gather her courage.

She got out her phone and messaged Debra.

I'm in New York. The hotel is nice. Thanks for always looking out for me. Miss you already. Wish you were here. Clem x

She did miss Deb. Being in New York with her would be a hoot. She sat down on the side of the bed, suddenly teary. What was she doing?

"What is it about this Sam that's so fantastic?" Deb had once snapped.

"We communicate well," Clementine said.

"Of course you communicate well, you idiot. It's all emails and texts and messages. I could come across as the Duchess of fucking Cambridge if I wanted. You don't see the real person that way."

"Well, I think you do," sniffed Clementine. "Long emails take time and energy and heart."

Debra rolled her eyes. "Excuse me while I puke!"

"It's love."

"You wouldn't know love if it bit you on the arse."

Debra was wrong. She did know love. And if she hurried, she'd meet it face to face within an hour.

Tilda

Vision is the art of seeing things invisible
Jonathan Swift

Five days before Christmas

It started with her finger.

Tilda was putting together a bouquet of seasonal flowers, berries and foliage for a wedding order when she noticed that her little finger was missing. She blinked a few times, unable to believe her eyes. But there was no denying it. Her finger was gone.

She dropped the bridal bouquet on the bench and fell into a nearby chair. The room swam around her. She panicked. She could feel her heart racing. *Breathe ... breathe ...* How could she lose a finger and not know?

It took her a few minutes to calm herself. Once she was able to, she held her hand up in front of her face. Gone. But there was no blood. No sign of an injury. No pain. Simply no finger.

She tried to remember the last time she'd looked at her hand. She'd used her hand without concern all morning. It was her right hand, so she'd used it constantly.

She'd used it to wave to Paige as she passed by the Happy Endings Bookshop. She'd used it to find her keys in her bag and then to open the door of her shop, the Flower Pot.

She'd answered the phone, taken some orders, checked her emails and her online orders. Surely if her finger had been missing then, she'd have noticed it?

Tilda wiggled her fingers, one by one. Her thumb. Check. Her index finger and then her rude finger, as her niece had called it when she was little. All good. Her ring-less finger, as she called it. Check. And then ... tentatively ... her little finger. Check.

What?

She could still feel it. It was there. She hadn't lost her little finger—she just couldn't see it.

Tilda stumbled through the shop to the bathroom out the back. She held the sink basin and stared into the mirror, searching her eyes. Was there a problem? Was she crazy? Surely even asking that question ruled it out.

Was she going blind? She looked over at the far wall and could read the small print on the sign she'd recently pinned to the toilet door: *Please don't use water from this bathroom for the showroom. You don't like to drink from the toilet and nor do our flowers.* Her niece, Debra, was twenty-two and worked with her now, but sometimes she was still a big kid and needed reminding about this.

The fact that she could read the sign gave her some comfort. Her eyes seemed fine. She turned back to the mirror and stared into them. There didn't seem to be any weird shadows or spots. Her eyes were as blue as ever. In fact, she'd forgotten how blue they were.

And then to her absolute horror ... Tilda noticed that her right ear was missing. As if in slow motion, she raised her hand—yes, the one missing the finger—to the side of her head and touched the spot where her ear used to be.

She could feel it. She gave her ear a tug. It was definitely still there. Her ear was still on her head. She just couldn't see it.

And with that, Tilda turned to the toilet and threw up.

*

Once she'd pulled herself together, Tilda closed the shop and walked the three blocks to her doctor's office. She needed to seek medical advice. It might be something quite minor. There was no point getting all worked up until she knew. Tilda was practical like that.

She used the walk to calm herself. It was a beautiful winter day. Cold, but the sun was shining. Muswell Hill was buzzing. The shops were draped in Christmas finery and filled with people buying presents. *Take that all, you naysayers who were predicting economic doom.*

She walked past a pair of young women in short skirts and long boots, talking a hundred miles an hour about their boyfriends. Heads turned as they passed, but they didn't notice. They were probably used to it.

Tilda was pleased to find the doctor's surgery quite empty. She waited at the front desk while the receptionist spoke to someone on the phone. Finally the receptionist hung up, but instead of turning to Tilda, she tidied up the paperwork in front of her. Eventually, Tilda coughed and the girl looked up.

"I'm sorry. I didn't see you there."

"I don't have an appointment, but I need to see Dr. Majumdar. It's quite urgent."

The girl glanced over at the computer screen. "We can fit you in now. Quiet morning. Must be the weather."

Tilda gave the receptionist her details and then took a seat in the waiting room. There was only one other patient before her: a man with a toddler strapped into his stroller. The father looked exhausted and didn't even glance her way, but the little boy did. He stopped trying to break free and stared at Tilda. She waved and he smiled back. She played peekaboo behind her hands, which set the child into a fit of giggles. His father absent-mindedly ruffled his hair and mumbled, "What are you laughing at?"

Half an hour later, Tilda was seated in Dr. Majumdar's office, trying to remember the last time she'd been there. Probably earlier in the year for her annual pap smear. She found those things dreadfully embarrassing, but they needed to be done. And she liked Dr. Majumdar. He always chatted to her about gardening or Indian spices, which took her mind off the task at hand. Plus he'd been the only doctor, out of three, who'd been able to diagnose her sesame seed allergy years ago, so she'd stuck with him.

"How can I help you today, Tilda?" His voice was like maple syrup and just as comforting.

"This is going to sound crazy but ... I can't see my little finger." Tilda slapped her hand onto his desk.

Dr. Majumdar peered at her hand over the rim of his glasses. "It does seem to be missing."

Tilda breathed a sigh of relief. "Oh thank god. Not that I've lost my finger. I'm extremely worried about that, but I'm so pleased you can see that it's missing too. That would rule out my eyes or my mental health."

"So it would seem." The doctor reached over and took her hand. He checked her fingers one by one, just as she had earlier, and then when he got to her little finger, gave it a good yank. "It's still there. Just invisible."

Tilda allowed him to state the obvious because she figured he was as shocked as she'd been.

"When did you first notice it missing?"

"About an hour ago. I definitely used that hand to open my shop, and set up for the day. And I didn't notice anything unusual then. However, I was working on a bridal bouquet, and that's when I saw it was gone." Tilda leaned forward and pushed her hair back off her face. "But that's not all. My ear is missing too."

Dr. Majumdar stared at the side of Tilda's head. She could see his mind was ticking over, just as it had when he diagnosed her sesame seed allergy. He gave her ear a yank, and then made a *mmm hphh* sound. Finally he sat back in his chair and rested his chin on his intertwined hands. And he stared at her.

Tilda shuffled in her seat and pretended to be interested in his bookcase. Then her nails ... on the nine fingers she could see.

"How old are you, Tilda?" The doctor grabbed his notepad and began jotting her answers down.

"Forty-five."

"Married?"

"Divorced."

"Children?"

"No, probably missed that boat, I'm afraid."

"When was the last time you had a boyfriend?"

Tilda was embarrassed by the questions. "I dated someone for three months last year. But it didn't work out."

"Why not?"

"I wasn't keen on him dating other women, and he was."

"Was he your last sexual partner?" His pen was poised.

"Yes, he was."

"Are your periods regular?"

"I guess. A few days out either side."

"Any hot flushes?"

"No." Apart from now, with all these embarrassing questions.

"I see." Dr. Majumdar stood. "Come over to the table, Tilda, and I'll examine you."

Tilda sat on the table while the doctor checked her reflexes, her heart, pulse and blood pressure. He did a breast check, and felt her glands. He looked inside her mouth and throat, and then her ears. He got her to stand and slowly turn around while he watched her. And then he led her back to her seat.

"Well, the good news is, you're not dying," he said.

Tilda placed a hand on her chest. "That's a relief. And the bad news?"

"You have invisibility."

"I'm sorry?"

"Invisibility. You're becoming invisible."

Tilda stared at the doctor, unable to speak. He continued, his voice kind but firm.

"It's quite common in women as they get older. You're a little young. Most women who suffer from invisibility notice the symptoms in their late forties, early fifties, but I had a patient recently who was still in her twenties. And that poor girl suffered a dreadful case of it. Woke up one morning and couldn't see her own head."

"I'm disappearing?"

"We don't use that term anymore. Women who suffer from invisibility don't literally disappear. That's just media hype."

"But people won't be able to see me?"

"Correct. In most cases. Though recent research shows that even patients with full-blown invisibility are still visible to some people."

"How can that be?"

"We don't know."

Tilda couldn't believe this was happening. "Is there a cure?"

"I'm afraid not." His tone was final.

"Any treatment?"

"There's no magic pill, if that's what you're asking. There are some trials being run by pharmaceutical companies, but nothing I'd recommend." He opened his desk drawer, shuffled through it for a moment, and then drew out a flyer. "There's a local support group that meets every week. The details are on here. You just show up. At least you're not alone."

Tilda looked into Dr. Majumdar's eyes. "What will I do?"

"You'll find ways to live with it, Tilda."

"I see."

"Yes, you will."

Tilda's brow furrowed. Had she missed something? "Sorry?"

Dr. Majumdar smiled kindly. "When you say '*I see*' ... that's the key. I've broken the same news to many patients. I've watched how they cope over the years. The ones who do well all have one thing in common."

"What's that, doctor?"

He looked at her over the rim of his glasses. "They all see things differently."

*

Tilda made her way back toward the shop. Everything seemed very different on the return walk. The sun wasn't as bright. People were rugged up and in a rush. She noticed now that a couple of the boutiques were empty. It was nearly Christmas but no one was spending money. *A sign of the depressed economy*, she thought.

Tilda's steps slowed and a young woman passed, not a care in the world. Tilda wondered if she was cold in her flimsy clothes.

She caught sight of herself in a shop window and paused. She had to look hard to even see herself. A sob caught in her throat, and she turned and ran all the way back down Broadway, past dozens of people who didn't notice her distress, and into the Happy Endings bookshop.

Paige saw her come in and immediately knew something was wrong. She called for her assistant Clementine to take over at the register and rushed straight over to Tilda, who was by this time sobbing into her hands. Paige grabbed Tilda's arm and led her out the back of the shop and upstairs to her apartment.

"Where we can have some privacy," Paige said.

Once inside, Paige held Tilda on the lounge while wracking sobs tore through her.

"Darling, has someone died?"

Tilda shook her head. "I've just been to see my doctor. I've been diagnosed with invisibility."

Paige's hand flew to her mouth. Her head shook in sympathy with her friend. "Oh, you poor thing. What a shock."

"I'm so sorry, Paige, barreling in like this."

"Don't be daft. Thank god you did. I'd hate to think you'd just go home alone." Paige handed Tilda some tissues.

"You've got enough on your plate with your mother," Tilda said.

"So it's nice to focus on someone else for a while." Paige said. "How about I make you a cup of tea and you tell me what happened."

Tilda smiled gratefully. "That would be lovely, thank you."

So Tilda told Paige the whole story, while her friend made tea, and then they sat and drank it and talked some more.

"Tilda, I'm not saying you were misdiagnosed, but I can see your finger," Paige told her.

"You can?"

"Absolutely. I'd never lie about something like that."

Tilda pulled her hair back. "What about my ear?"

Paige's face fell. "Oh … you're right, that is missing." She patted Tilda's knee. "You're strong, darling. You'll get through this."

"I don't have much choice, do I?"

"No, but you have support. Me, Eva … Let's catch a movie this week."

"I'll see how I go, Paige. I might need a few days to absorb this."

"You get two days," Paige teased. "After that we'll come and find you."

"Not if you can't see me." Tilda gave Paige a wry smile. She could feel herself gathering strength, just talking to her friend. "I'm shocked at the moment, but I'm already determined to gather as much information as possible on invisibility. There must be some sort of treatment out there."

"I've had a few customers with invisibility," Paige said. "They come in looking for books on it."

"Do you have any?"

"I have an excellent one. Apparently it's the must-read book for sufferers." Paige stood and took their cups back into the kitchen. "Come and I'll get it for you."

They returned to the bookstore and Paige found the book for Tilda.

The Invisible Women: From Cloak to Cape, by Selma Nester.

"It's a gift. You have it," Paige said.

Tilda wouldn't hear of it. "Absolutely not. I'll buy it."

"Rubbish, I was wondering what to get you for Christmas anyway. I saw a lovely pair of earrings—" Paige slapped her hand across her mouth. "Oh shit, I'm sorry."

The two women looked at each other in horror, and then Tilda began to giggle. Eventually, Paige joined her. The laughter got louder until they were doubled over, in the middle of the Happy Endings bookstore.

"Oh, darling, at least you have your sense of humor," Paige howled.

"I promise you, that'll be the last thing that disappears," Tilda said.

*

Tilda couldn't face going back to her shop. She decided to take a few more hours off, so called Debra to keep an eye on things.

"Deb, where are you?"

"I'm just pulling up at the shop. Where the hell are you?"

Tilda was a bit thrown by Debra's intensity. "I have some business to take care of."

"The same business that would have you sobbing down at Happy Endings? Clem called and said you were hysterical. What's going on?"

Tilda sighed. Clementine and Debra shared a flat and were best friends. "I'm fine. I just need a few hours off."

"Do you have cancer?"

"I don't have cancer."

That seemed to appease Debra. "Okay. I'll see you when you get back." And she hung up.

Tilda never took time off, so it was no wonder Debra thought something was wrong. And then Tilda remembered something *was* wrong. She was becoming invisible.

She went into her favorite cafe, found a vacant table at the back and ordered a flat white. Then she opened the book Paige had given her.

So you've been diagnosed with invisibility. You're not alone, it's just you can't see the others. Invisibility is more common than we realize. Statistics show that 70 percent of women over fifty suffer some form of invisibility. While a small percentage of women have appendages, limbs and sometimes their whole body vanish, more often than not they only suffer from mild symptoms, which go undiagnosed. Many women remain completely visible physically, and yet spend years missing out on career and social opportunities because of the emotional impact their mild invisibility has on them.

This insidious disorder is not a modern-day dilemma, as most in the medical profession would have you believe. It has been around for centuries.

Leading invisibility academic Olivia Lurkan spent her career deciphering coded mentions of the disorder in the Bible, and later wrote about it in her bestselling book, I've Got No Limbs.

I too was diagnosed with invisibility. I lost the whole right side of my body before I discovered the key to beating this horrible disease. Since then, I have dedicated my life to helping other women beat it. Because here's what no doctor will tell you: Invisibility is a curable condition. And you can start right now.

Tilda flicked over a couple of pages. Who was this woman? Dr. Majumdar had told her that there was no cure for invisibility, and she certainly trusted him. She found the author biography.

Selma Nester has a PhD in psychology from Wroclaw University. Her work in the field of invisibility and female disappearing disorders is renowned. In 1997 she was awarded the Eastern European Prize for Women's Health. Selma has a private practice in Hampstead, London. She was diagnosed with invisibility in 1987. By 1992 she was completely visible again.

Tilda stared at the photos attached to the biography. One photo was taken in 1989 and was of a rather mousy-looking woman with one side of her body missing. The second photo was from three years ago. While much older, the woman in that photograph was clearly visible.

A ray of hope! Elated, Tilda slammed her book shut. She needed to absorb what she'd read.

"Quite a book, eh?"

Tilda realized the man at the next table was speaking to her.

"You slammed that book shut like someone who just made a wonderful discovery in it," he said. "Next you'll drink your coffee and think about it."

Tilda politely smiled. "You can tell all that just from how I closed my book?"

"I like to read between the lines."

Tilda looked at the stranger for a moment. He was about her age, perhaps a little younger, with tousled brown hair and a pleasant face. More than pleasant, although that was difficult to tell at first glance because he was wearing sunglasses.

Probably trying to be cool, thought Tilda. Although he didn't look like someone who would try to be cool, or anything else. He was friendly, and eager to chat.

"Do you come here a lot?"

Tilda's eyes narrowed. "This is a cafe, not a bar."

The man laughed. "Does that mean I won't get that whiskey I just ordered?"

Tilda smiled. His warmth was disarming. "To answer your question, yes, I do come here a lot. I'm a regular. I own the florist next door."

"That would explain the smell of snowdrops when you walked in."

Tilda was completely taken aback. "Are you a bloodhound?"

"Only when there's a full moon."

"I just received a large order of snowdrops this morning. Are you a gardener?"

"No, just a loyal grandson. My grandmother is obsessed with her garden and I do my best to appear interested."

"I suspect you do a good job of it."

Tilda felt her guard coming down. This man was not only handsome, and nice ... but he was talking to her. He'd instigated a conversation with her.

Take that, invisibility!

"How about you? Do you work around here?" she asked.

"Not far from here," he said. "I'm a music teacher."

"What do you teach?"

"Piano, viola, and violin. A little piano accordion."

Tilda was impressed. "You're so lucky. I always wish I'd learned to play an instrument."

"It's never too late."

Tilda shook her head. "At my age … I couldn't."

"What's age got to do with it? I have a new student who just turned ninety. She'd always wanted to learn piano and figured she'd better get to it before she got too old."

Tilda glanced down at her missing finger. Hardly a good time for piano lessons now. "Well, I'll keep it in mind."

"Things never get done when they're kept there."

He'd lost her. "Kept where?"

"In mind. When you say, 'I'll keep it in mind,' that's usually where it stays."

Tilda was a little uncomfortable with the conversation she was having with this stranger, so she turned the talk back to him. "Do you also work as a musician?"

"I do. Session work mainly. I'm in a band, but that's for love, not money." He smiled at her and Tilda noticed how lovely his teeth were.

"You should come and hear us play sometime," he said.

"I'll keep an eye out for you."

"Or an ear."

"Right."

He reached his hand across the table and without hesitation Tilda thrust hers out and took it. His finger were long, his hand smooth yet strong.

"I'm Patrick."

"Tilda."

"What a great name."

Tilda blushed. It had been quite a long time since a man had paid her a compliment. She suddenly felt warmer than she'd felt all winter.

"As much as I've enjoyed chatting, Tilda, I have a lesson to get to." Patrick stood and gathered his bag. Then, to her horror, he picked up a white cane.

"I'll be seeing you, Tilda."

It was as much as she could do to stutter out, "Nice to meet you, Patrick."

And with that he made his way over to the register, where Tilda watched him chat to the waitress and pay for his drink. Then, tapping the cane in front of him, he turned and left the cafe with more grace than she'd ever been able to muster despite having full sight.

Tilda sat quietly for a moment. A painful knot had formed in her gut. She felt so stupid. She thought he'd seen her and had found her appealing enough to talk to. But no, he was no doubt the type of man who struck up conversations with strangers all the time. Didn't blind people have heightened senses? He could probably smell her desperation, along with the snowdrops, and was just being nice.

The waitress appeared and started wiping down the table. She stopped mid-wipe. "Oh, sorry, love, I thought you'd left."

"I'm just coming to pay now."

"No need. Patrick paid for yours."

Tilda blanched. Would he claim that on his tax? Annual charity contributions: Bought a coffee for an invisible woman. "Does he do that a lot?"

"Nope." The waitress gave the table in front of Tilda a quick swipe and walked off.

*

148

The following morning, Tilda's whole hand was missing. She was still able to use it, but she couldn't see it. Aware that she couldn't take more time off, and conscious of frightening her customers, she dug some gloves out of her drawer and wore them.

Once in the shop she opened *The Invisible Woman* again.

There are many physical, emotional, intellectual and spiritual reasons why a woman will manifest invisibility, and these reasons will determine the type of treatment she receives. There is no truth to the information out there about the link between invisibility and dairy products. In all my years of studying this disorder, I have seen no evidence that it is linked to diet.

All the evidence I have gathered points to one factor first and foremost: every woman who has beaten this disorder has been proactive. Everyone has the desire to heal, but that's not enough. Motivation is the key. Every single woman I have treated and cured of this condition has been proactive right from the start. Are you?

Proactive? Was she proactive? The invisibility disorder was recent, so she hadn't yet had time to be proactive. Whatever that meant. It was one of those words bandied about at corporate motivation seminars. If she needed to be proactive, first she'd have to find out what that meant. She jumped online and did a search.

Proactive: Initiating change rather than simply responding to events after they have occurred.

Right. That's what she thought it meant. It's just she'd never thought about it in connection to her life, or the way she lived her life. When had she been proactive about anything?

Perhaps her divorce. She'd instigated that, although it hadn't been hard. She'd married too young and it simply hadn't worked out. The end was more relief than heartache, for both of them.

When had she initiated change? She'd taken over the Flower Pot when the original owner retired. Although that also didn't take much effort. It was where she'd trained and worked for years, so all it took was a small bank loan and some courage. It had been a practical move. She loved her work and it provided a decent enough income that she had been able to not only survive but also stash away a nest egg for retirement.

Perhaps her nest egg was proactive. It was certainly sensible.

What else? She took a daily multivitamin. Did that count?

She wasn't much of a go-getter, but was that wrong? She had her routine, but wasn't unhappy. Was she? Tilda couldn't ever remember asking herself that question. She just got on with life.

Tilda turned back to the computer and did a search for Selma Nester. There were thousands of pages, but right at the top was her website. And what a website it was. There were YouTube clips of Selma on *Oprah*. There were testimonials from Deepak Chopra and Trinny and Susannah. *Time* magazine once had her on the cover.

She must be doing something right.

Tilda found the office contact, and without thinking it through too much, she dialed the number.

"Visibility Centre."

"Hello, I'm calling to make an appointment with Dr. Nester."

The receptionist was brisk and efficient. "Have you seen her before?"

"No."

"We're currently taking appointments for November next year."

So much for being proactive. A sob caught in Tilda's throat. "That's nearly twelve months away. I might be completely invisible by then."

The receptionist paused for a moment and then in a kind voice asked, "Have you just been diagnosed, love?"

"I have, yes."

"You sound quite young."

"Forty-five."

Tilda could hear the receptionist tutting to herself.

"Look, I'm not meant to do this, because there's a wait list, but there is a cancellation for tomorrow morning at nine. Want it?"

"You would do that for me?"

"My dear, be grateful for these moments, but not so surprised. Not if you want to heal."

Tilda wasn't quite sure what the woman meant, but she couldn't deny how relieved she felt. "I'll take it. Thank you so much."

The receptionist gave Tilda the appointment details and Tilda hung up feeling incredibly proactive. Next, she grabbed her bag and pulled out the flyer for the invisibility support group.

Have you been diagnosed with invisibility? Feel all alone? People might not be able to see you, but this group of people will hear you. Come and share your story, your pain, every Friday at 1 pm. We are "hear" for you!

Friday at 1 pm? That was today. Tilda glanced at the clock: the meeting was just three hours away. She could close for lunch and go along. She already felt a lot better—like she was in charge, not her disorder. It was going to be a good day, she knew it.

Right on cue, the door jangled and in walked Patrick. In one hand he had his cane, in the other a beautiful bouquet of white orchids.

"Patrick?"

"Hi, Tilda. I thought you'd like these."

Tilda felt stunned and was grateful he couldn't see that. Was he nuts? "You brought me flowers?"

"Being a florist, I figured you must like them a lot."

Good point. "I do."

"Then you'll love these." Patrick thrust them toward her. "Smell them."

Tilda did as she was told.

"Aren't they glorious?"

She had to agree. "Where did you find them, Patrick?" She felt a stab of jealousy that she wasn't the one selling them.

"They're from my grandmother's hothouse."

"They're beautiful. I'm touched."

Tilda and Patrick stood and looked at each other for a moment. Or rather, she looked at him. She had no idea what he saw, if anything, and would never dream of asking. She had a tendency to skirt around issues or pretend they didn't exist. She'd never been the type to just confront something.

"Are you completely blind?" What had come over her?

"I'm legally blind, if that's what you're asking."

"So you can't see anything at all?"

"That's not the best question to ask. Why don't you ask what I *can* see?"

Tilda wished the floor would swallow her. What had gotten into her? "I'm so sorry, Patrick. It's dreadfully rude of me."

Patrick smiled. "Tilda, you're not being rude. I understand you're curious. To answer your question, I can see some light. Some shadows, too—but nothing defined."

"Were you born blind?" Another question she wouldn't ordinarily ask.

"No. I was diagnosed with retinitis pigmentosa when I was seven years old. My sight got progressively worse. By fourteen I had tunnel vision and night blindness. By twenty, I was seeing the world through a straw."

"I see." Tilda could kick herself for her choice of words, but Patrick seemed to sense that and laughed.

"It's okay, Tilda. I don't get offended every time you use that word."

"I feel like I make a fool of myself every time I speak to you."

"Let's work on that. Have dinner with me tonight."

Tilda was shocked. No one had asked her out for ages. Did he feel sorry for her?

Patrick gave her a very sexy smile. "The benefit of being blind right now is that I can't see the look on your face."

"I'm sure it's idiotic," Tilda said. "Patrick, you might not ask me out if ..." She paused. Could her foot be shoved any further down her throat?

"If I could see you?" He seemed more amused than offended. "Are you butt ugly, Tilda?"

Tilda had to laugh. "I ... er ... no. I mean, I'm no supermodel, but ... I'm all right. It's just you don't know me."

"The crazy thing about first dates is that it gives two people a chance to rectify that."

"I'm forty-five and I look it," she blurted.

"I'm forty-two and I have no idea how I look."

Tilda had to laugh. He made her laugh. And he was nice. And handsome. She wanted to go out to dinner with him. There was absolutely no reason why she shouldn't go out with him.

Tilda chose her words carefully this time. "I'd love to have dinner with you, Patrick. I close here at six."

He beamed. "I'll meet you here then."

"I look forward to it." And once again, the sight analogy made her cringe.

*

The meeting for the invisibility support group was held at the local community hall. Thanks to a rather complicated wreath for a funeral, Tilda was running a few minutes late. She entered the room and a woman missing the whole bottom part of her body floated over to her.

"I often wonder if Michael Jackson suffered it, you know." The woman gave Tilda a knowing look. "It's rare in men, but he had the signs."

Tilda had no idea what she was talking about, and it showed.

"The glove," the woman explained, and looked down at Tilda's hands. "It often starts with the hand and we all wear gloves. As if that will make a difference."

Oh right! "I don't want to scare my customers."

"There's no getting around it. You'll eventually scare someone. Mine started in my hand as well, and now look at me."

Tilda did as she was told, even though she found looking at the woman rather disturbing.

"If that doesn't frighten people, what will?" The woman jutted her chin out to emphasize the point. "I'm Norma. Come and I'll introduce you to the others."

Tilda followed Norma into the room. There were about a dozen chairs in a circle. Some were taken. Other women milled around a table with tea and biscuits.

"Ladies, we have a new member today." Norma turned to Tilda. "I'm sorry, I didn't catch your name."

"Tilda."

The other women nodded and murmured their greetings.

Norma motioned for Tilda to join the circle. "We're about to start, so if you'd like to take a seat."

Tilda made her way over to the chairs. She was just about to sit in one when another woman stopped her.

"Carol is sitting there."

The empty chair spoke. "Not a problem. Happens all the time."

Tilda was aghast Poor Carol was completely invisible. She moved up a seat, next to a woman who didn't have any specific limb missing, but just looked generally hazy. She introduced herself, but Tilda had to blink a lot to keep her in focus.

"I'm Sheila. Just diagnosed?"

Tilda nodded. "Yesterday."

"I've been suffering it for fifteen years."

Tilda looked shocked. "You don't look old enough."

"That's very kind, but I'm forty-five."

"Me too." Tilda swallowed the urge to scream, *And that's not old!* Instead she turned to the rest of the group, who were now seated.

Norma ran the group. Tilda had the feeling that Norma ran a lot of things. She looked efficient. She was rather stocky, with the kind of severe short hairdo that wearers often thought of as 'practical'. Tilda made a mental note to wear her hair down more often.

"Perhaps we should start with Tilda," Norma said. "She can share her pain and suffering and then we can go around the circle and share ours with her." Norma gave everyone a smile that didn't reach her eyes. "Tilda, all yours."

Tilda disliked speaking in front of groups, but, remembering her decision to be proactive, she forged ahead.

"I'm still absorbing my diagnosis. It's been a shock."

Everyone nodded in sympathy.

"I'm trying to understand what it means for me."

Another group nod. The sympathy was fairly dripping from the walls.

"But I intend to do everything I can to heal myself."

There was an intake of air. The other members glanced at each other, then turned to Norma, who snickered.

Tilda fought the urge to slap her. "Did I say something funny?"

Norma spoke with patronizing concern. "Not funny, just uninformed. I hear this so often, just after diagnosis. Women who think they can somehow beat this."

"You don't think I can?"

"I have suffered this dreadful disease for many years now. I'm pretty sure if there was an effective treatment for it, I'd have heard about it."

"I've been reading a book by Selma Nester—"

This time a few of the other women tittered along with Norma.

"That woman is a charlatan," Norma said. "I went to her once and she barely even discussed my disorder. Instead we had a ridiculous conversation about my haircut."

Tilda bit down on her lip to stop herself from smiling.

"I wanted to know if an antidepressant would help me cope. But she asked too many questions and never answered any. She was very rude."

Tilda refrained from mentioning her own appointment with Dr. Nester and let Norma continue.

"You're still reeling from the shock of diagnosis, Tilda. You might even be a little delusional."

Tilda raised an eyebrow but kept her mouth shut. Her body might be disappearing but her mind was fine. Apart from the vision she suddenly had of pushing Norma into a vat of acid. Perhaps Norma was right and she was mad after all.

Norma had the floor and worked it. "This is the reality of invisibility. I have some lovely trousers, but feel extremely despondent because no one can see them once I put them on. I might as well be naked from the waist down."

Tilda couldn't help herself. "Are you?"

Norma looked horrified. "Absolutely not. I'm wearing classic cut navy trousers from Marks & Spencer."

"I imagine it would be a bit nippy going naked, but you could probably get away with fleece tights and no one would know," Tilda said.

"A woman must keep certain standards." Norma gave her mustard-colored cardigan a little tug, as if to emphasize that fact.

"Why is it that I can see my glove but not your trousers?"

Norma nodded. This was evidently a much more appropriate question. "This is one of the mysteries of this insidious condition. Basically, invisibility affects the actual body first. Sufferers can get away with wearing clothes that mask the issue, as you're doing today with your glove. Over time, though, some victims find that their clothes also disappear." Norma waved a hand at Carol. "Carol favors tweed suits and gold jewelry but none of that can be seen."

"I'm still in my pajamas today." Carol's voice came from nowhere. "What's the point?"

Norma stared at the empty chair in frustration. "But I waited for you to get dressed when I came to pick you up."

"I had a brandy instead."

"Would you like to share your week with the group, Carol?"

"No ... I have nothing else to say."

Norma turned to the others. "Let Carol's deterioration be a lesson for us all."

Carol was silent, but the others couldn't wait to tell their stories. Jenny could barely get out of bed, she was so depressed about losing her arms. Cath was inconsolable because the automatic doors at the supermarket wouldn't open for her. Next came Lynda, who cried because she'd had to give her dog away. The poor animal couldn't see her anymore and wouldn't stop howling for her. Kate's missing head frightened her grandchildren. Lisa was thinking of giving up her work as a bus driver because people were refusing to get on her bus.

"Everyone thinks it's haunted," she wept.

And the whole time Tilda clutched the edge of her plastic chair and fought the urge to scream at them. They were so negative. Was this her future? Wasn't there a glimmer of light anywhere? Wasn't there a positive story to share? Surely something funny had happened to one of them? If this was a support group, where was the laughter? Wasn't *that* the best medicine?

But then, who was she to judge? Perhaps years of living with invisibility had worn them down. Tilda tried to have some empathy for these women, but felt suffocated by their lethargy and pessimism. They howled and moaned and cried and by the end of the meeting Tilda felt completely despondent.

After the meeting, Norma gave her an awkward hug. "Doesn't it feel good to know that you're not alone? We'll see you at the next meeting." It was a statement, not a question.

"That sounds great." Tilda walked out of the hall vowing never to return.

*

Tilda went straight home and had a shower. She felt like she needed to wash the support group meeting off. Was she like those women? True, life had become rather beige over the past few years, but she didn't see herself as a negative person. In fact, pessimism had always bothered her. So had optimism. She considered herself to be somewhere in the middle. She was pragmatic. Practical.

She soaped herself up as she always did: automatically. But something caused her to pause, and look down at her body. One of her breasts and part of her stomach were looking hazy. Were they disappearing now too?

Trying to look on the bright side, something she was determined to do after the meeting, she figured if her stomach disappeared that would at least help assuage her guilt every time she ate chocolate. She'd always been slim, but during the past couple of years a few extra pounds had crept up around her middle and it was impossible to lose them.

She felt much better after her shower. Despite the fact that she knew Patrick couldn't see her, Tilda still wanted to look nice for their date, so she took the opportunity to change into fresh clothes. She chose a skirt, and a turtleneck jumper. It was hardly the height of fashion, but she looked nice. She left her hair hanging loose, something she rarely did anymore. She wrapped a scarf around her neck and put on her favorite boots. She gave herself a squirt of perfume and then checked herself out in the mirror.

To her absolute mortification her nose was missing.

She was about to fall into a sobbing heap when she remembered … Patrick wouldn't know. He wouldn't notice her nose, or her ear. He wouldn't notice the grays that were sprouting up through her faded blonde locks. He certainly wouldn't notice the worn cuff on her sweater, or the fact that her boots had seen better days. She stared at her reflection with a mixture of pity and loathing, before a glimmer of something else surfaced. Defiance.

"You will not cancel."

She grabbed her bag and walked out the door.

"You will not cancel."

She repeated this mantra to herself until Patrick picked her up from the shop three hours later.

*

Patrick arrived more handsome than ever in jeans, a black shirt and leather jacket. He was wearing tinted glasses instead of the other darker ones. Walking beside him, Tilda appreciated for the first time just how tall he was. She liked tall men.

They got off to a slightly bumpy start when she tried to help him across the road.

"Tilda, I can manage."

Tilda pulled her hand away. "I'm sorry."

"How about we walk together, rather than one of us leading?"

And off he went. Before long, Tilda forgot about his cane and concentrated on him. He knew where he was going: a little Italian joint up the road. He moved with ease. And the whole time he made comments about what was going on around them, the sounds and smells of the evening, trying to set her at ease too. "Beautiful twilight weather. I love this time of night. Can you hear the carolers?" (She hadn't until he mentioned it.) They strolled on, and finally, as he held the door to the restaurant open for her, he said, 'I love the shampoo you use, Tilda. Is that jasmine?'

Patrick seemed to be a regular at Villaggio Italiano. He knew everyone in the room. People called out to him and he greeted them all by name as he recognized their voices. He made his way to a table in the back corner, and once seated, passed Tilda a menu.

"I eat here a lot so they know what I'll order."

"Do you frequent the same places because of your disability?"

Patrick looked at her in mock horror. "Do I have a disability?" Then he laughed. "I come to this restaurant regularly for the same reason sighted people do. It's good."

Tilda buried her head in the menu and was grateful he couldn't see her face burning. "The scaloppine ai funghi looks delicious."

"Good choice."

"Patrick, I just want to say that I'm very happy to be here with you and I hope I don't balls it up by saying the wrong thing all the time."

"Me too." He laughed again. "Tilda, I have no problem with you being curious about how I get around. Often people never talk about it at all." He leaned forward slightly, and spoke as though he was sharing a secret. "With some people I can almost hear them thinking, 'Don't mention the blindness,' as though they'd be the ones breaking it to me."

Tilda giggled.

He ran his hand across the table to the breadbasket in the center and took a piece. "Any other questions before we move on?"

She did have one. "Yes. How do you manage to look so ... handsome?"

"You think I'm handsome?"

Now she was really embarrassed. "I mean your clothes."

"So you don't think I'm handsome?"

Her cheeks burned. "I ... well, yes, you are very handsome."

"That's good to know. I haven't seen myself for years, so things might've changed."

Tilda laughed. "What I'm trying to say, rather inarticulately, is how do you know what to wear? You look very put-together."

Patrick cocked his head to one side, amused. "You want to know how I can leave the house wearing something reasonably coordinated?"

"Yes. I find that difficult and I can see."

"I stick to certain styles. I have labels attached to my shirts, so I know what color they are. I wear these glasses at night, because I don't need as much protection from light then. And I'm told they look trendy."

Tilda laughed. "They're very stylish."

"I'm flattered." He gave her one of his sexy grins. "I think you're gorgeous too."

"Oh, that's ... well ..." Tilda wiped some imaginary crumbs off the tablecloth.

"You don't believe me when I compliment you because I'm blind?"

"Patrick, it's clear that my foot-in-mouth is more of a problem than your blindness, but still … you don't know what I look like."

"True. But you're wearing a skirt tonight, and shoes with a heel. You're probably blonde, with shoulder-length hair. I know you're shorter than me. And slim."

He was very astute. Although he hadn't picked up on her invisible nose or ear.

"Why did you ask me out, Patrick?"

"For the same reason anyone asks anyone out."

Tilda was stumped.

"Because I find you attractive, Tilda." He shook his head, amazed she didn't get it. "Apart from the picture I have of you in my mind, I also liked the way you slammed that book shut. I liked the sound of your voice the first time we spoke. The slight scent of flowers that surrounds you."

Tilda was grateful he couldn't see the tears in her eyes. "But you can't see me."

"On the contrary," he said. "I see you clearly."

*

Tilda sat in Selma Nester's empty consultation room, tapping her foot nervously. The receptionist had told her that Dr. Nester wouldn't be long. The room was bright and airy, filled with photos of Selma with various female celebrities and politicians. There was a photo of her with Hillary Clinton, another with Madonna and Margaret Thatcher.

Tilda took the time to rewind over her date. Once she'd gotten over her fear of offending Patrick each time she opened her mouth, she'd enjoyed every minute of it. They'd talked and talked and Patrick had her in stitches over some of his stories about his students.

"How do you read music, Patrick?"

"Louis Braille also created a Braille system for notes. That's what I teach to students at the school I work at. But I use that as the foundation of my teachings. Music is something you feel and hear, not something you see. It's an invisible art form."

Tilda found him so attractive. He was well educated, well traveled, and … well, sexy. She forgot all about his blindness until he pulled out his wallet to pay for dinner, and she noticed how the notes were folded, each one in a different shape so he knew what it was worth.

Afterward, he walked her back to her shop.

"Next time, I'll walk you home, Tilda. I'll just need to get my bearings beforehand."

"I'm not far from here anyway." Tilda was fine with this arrangement, as she didn't want to be in a situation where she felt obliged to invite him in. She'd had a confusing week, and her growing feelings for Patrick only added to that.

"I had a great night, Tilda."

"So did I, Patrick."

"Can I see you again?" he asked. "How about tomorrow?"

And so they made plans for a second date. And then … he reached out and touched her face. It was such a tender gesture that Tilda almost cried. He seemed to sense this, and pulled her in close for one brief but delicious kiss. For a few seconds she forgot that she was disappearing, and thought she might disappear into him instead.

She drew breath. She could smell the faint traces of wine and an after-dinner mint on him … and something else on his breath. Something familiar. Something she wanted to deeply inhale, over and over again.

Suddenly the door swung open and Tilda slammed back to reality as the most vibrant-looking woman Tilda had ever seen marched into the consulting room. She was short, with bright red hair, striking clothes and intense dark eyes.

"Tilda … sorry to keep you waiting. Although you're probably used to it at your age."

Tilda nodded. She was right.

"I'm Selma, but you already know that."

Selma seated herself in a red chair opposite Tilda. Her head tilted to one side while she looked Tilda up and down. "My dear girl, when were you diagnosed?"

"This has all been rather sudden."

"Bad news always is."

"True."

"You've lost your nose."

"Yes," Tilda said, "and my hand, my ear, and now this morning my left foot has gone."

Selma's eyes shot down to Tilda's feet. "Well no wonder, in those shoes."

Tilda opened her mouth to say something, but stopped. Instead, she glanced at her shoes. They had seen better days, but they were comfy.

The intense eyes locked on Tilda. "So what's going on?"

Tilda had a feeling Selma was not interested in the long version of events. "I was diagnosed a couple of days ago. I've started reading your book. I read the chapter about being pro-active, so I made this appointment."

"That's a step forward."

"I also went to a support meeting in Muswell Hill."

"And three steps back." Selma gave a snort. "Is that the one run by Norma?"

"Yes."

"Sweet Jesus, did you feel like throwing yourself under a bus afterward?"

Tilda liked Selma already. "It crossed my mind."

Selma leaned forward slightly in her chair. "You get what you focus on, Tilda. Those women focus on the invisibility. It's no wonder we can't see them." Selma took a notepad and pen off the table beside her. "Do you ever wear make-up?"

"A little. When I go out."

"How would you describe your wardrobe?"

"I used to be quite quirky, but I don't think that's appropriate over forty, so I'm a bit lost at the moment."

Selma's eyes flared at her. "Who says it's not appropriate to be quirky over forty?"

"I don't know. Magazines. My mother."

"Is your mother a frump?"

"Er ... she's conservative." Tilda wasn't sure where this line of questioning was headed.

"So you ditched your old style when you turned forty, but still haven't found the new you?" Selma glanced at her notes. "It says here that you're forty-five. That's a long time to be in limbo, with no outward way to express yourself."

"Are you suggesting appearance matters?"

"Of course it matters."

Tilda had always prided herself on not getting caught up in all the propaganda pumped out by women's magazines. "Don't you think it's unhealthy to focus on appearance?"

"No, I don't." Selma stared at Tilda as if to challenge her. "It's unhealthy to focus solely on appearance. It's unhealthy to dress for others. But, my dear girl, it's extremely healthy to do what it takes to feel good about yourself. And you can choose how you do that. I have a lot of clients who are beating this disorder. One of them couldn't give a rat's arse about nice clothes. She looks like a bag lady. But she values a good cut and color. Another client has regular massages. Another has a weekly manicure. None of these women are superficial.

But they feel good about themselves on a superficial level. And that's an excellent place to start."

"I see."

"What do you see?" Selma raised her pen, ready to jot down Tilda's answer.

"I see that I have got rather complacent about how I look."

"It's not an easy age, Tilda. The symbolic annihilation of women by the media is so complete that the media's not even the enemy anymore. We are our own worst enemies." Selma sniffed, showing her distaste.

Tilda stared at Selma wondering how old she was. She had wrinkles, and creases, and lines. But she was beautiful. Her eyes sparkled, and her face had life and laughter written all over it. Her zest for living was clearly apparent. Tilda figured she must be in her seventies or even eighties, but she seemed ageless.

"So what do you suggest?" Tilda asked.

"Women need to stop clutching at the remnants of their youth and fully embrace ageing." Selma waved her arms around theatrically. "We should *welcome* ageing. It's a privilege denied to many."

"I don't understand. On the one hand you're saying I should accept growing old, on the other hand you're saying I need a makeover. Perhaps I need Botox too?"

Selma looked like she'd been slapped. "There's a difference between being in denial about your age, and embracing it with some fabulous clothes and a great haircut."

Tilda touched the side of her hair. She couldn't deny feeling great whenever she did take time to get a cut and color.

"Growing old doesn't mean giving up," Selma said. She looked back down at her notes. "Do you work?"

"I'm a florist. I have a small store."

"Like it?" Selma asked.

"Yes, I do."

"Kids?"

"No. Is that common with women who have invisibility?"

"I've seen a few, but I see way more women in here with kids. It seems to be especially prevalent in women with teenage daughters." Back to her notes. "Do you exercise?"

"I don't go to the gym or anything, but I walk a lot."

"Any hobbies? Any interests."

"Ah ... I like reading."

"What type of books?"

"I read a lot of books on gardening, and I have a soft spot for romance. In fact I belong to a book club. We meet regularly and I enjoy that."

Selma nodded her head approvingly. "How do you treat yourself?"

Tilda thought for a moment. She used to enjoy treating herself to weekends in Paris, but it had been ages since she'd done that. Certainly not since she'd taken over the business.

"I don't."

"You don't?" Selma looked at Tilda as if she was speaking Swahili.

"Perhaps I used to treat myself when I was younger. Trips away. New clothes. I don't know. I just haven't thought about it for a long time."

Selma drew back in disbelief. "It's time you did. Don't you agree?"

"Does it help fight invisibility?"

"Have you read my whole book?"

"Not yet, but I will," said Tilda apologetically.

"If invisibility were a color, it would be beige. To combat it, we must color the world around us." Selma's voice lowered slightly. "Do you have a partner?"

"No."

"When was the last time you had sex?"

Tilda tried to remember. "It's been a while." She thought about Patrick. She'd like to have sex with him. "I've just met someone. We went out to dinner last night."

Selma flashed her a smile. "Lovely. Is he nice?"

"Very."

"Excellent."

"But he's blind."

"In what way?"

Tilda was a bit thrown by Selma's question. "He can't see."

"Oh, is that all? I thought you meant really blind."

"He is *really* blind. He can't see."

Selma appeared frustrated by Tilda. "What does it mean to see? To truly see? Look at this world we live in. Everyone is blind. Dear girl, you're as blind as a bat or you wouldn't be here."

"What do you mean I'm blind?

"You've lost sight. Of yourself. And if you can't see yourself, how will anyone else?"

*

Tilda could barely concentrate on work after her session with Selma. It had stirred up more questions than it had answered, mostly about her appearance.

"I'm not one to obsess about clothes or fashion," she'd told Selma.

"This isn't about *fashion*. Fashion isn't important. Personal style is."

"Fine, then my style is to ignore ... style."

Selma gave an amused snort. "Oh, you're such a rebel. If that was the truth, then good for you, but we both know it's not. Helena Bonham Carter carries that off. You, my dear, are lost."

Tilda stared straight ahead. She had nothing to say to that. It was the unfortunate truth.

"Make clear sartorial choices," said Selma. "Style is not about following trends, or even starting them ... It's about being yourself. And for god's sake, dear, don't listen to your mother, or magazines, or anyone else, about what is appropriate to wear at your age. There are no rules. If you find yourself following some, then you're way off track."

Time was up and Selma led Tilda to the door.

"Know who you are and express it—physically, emotionally, intellectually and spiritually." Selma had looked at her, one dramatic eyebrow raised. "We've only touched on the external today, Tilda. Imagine when we get down to the real work."

Standing at her shop window, Tilda shuddered at the thought. She looked out, watching the world pass by. Did all of these strangers know who they were? Or had they lost sight of themselves as well?

A woman of about fifty walked by with a shopping bag.

A teenage girl strutted by with a boy her own age nipping at her heels like an eager pup.

A couple hurried past holding hands.

An old woman walked by slowly with her head held high. She was taking her time, and at one point she paused, and lifted her face to the sun and smiled.

How lovely she looked, thought Tilda. And then she noticed the woman's shoes. They were red, with a small heel.

Tilda looked down at her own shoes. Selma was right. They were dreadful. Unless you were milking cows, there was no excuse for such footwear.

Tilda grabbed her bag and keys and turned the sign on the shop door: *Back in ten minutes*. Then she headed toward a little shoe shop nearby that she'd noticed but never bothered to enter.

The shelves were filled with beautiful winter shoes. She examined the loafers and pumps and boots of varying lengths, then ran her hand across a beautiful pair of red stilettos. Although breathtaking, they weren't practical. But she smiled when she thought of the old lady with the red shoes. Then she saw them: a gorgeous pair of black ankle boots. They had a heel, but not too high.

Tilda turned to the girl who worked there. "Can I try these on in a seven?"

The girl glanced at Tilda's shoes. "Absolutely," she said as she disappeared out the back. She emerged a couple of minutes later with two shoeboxes.

She handed Tilda the first box. "These are the boots." And then she opened the second box and drew out a beautiful and very simple tan flat. "I thought you might like to try these on as well. They've just come in."

Tilda hesitated. She disliked pushy sales assistants, but the pump was lovely. It wasn't unlike the shoe she was wearing. It was as if her shoe was the unfashionable country bumpkin and this shoe was the classy city cousin.

Tilda took the shoe. "Thank you."

She tried the boot on first. It fit like a glove. She glanced briefly at the sales assistant and then removed her other old shoe, hearing a small gasp when the girl noticed Tilda's missing foot. Tilda ignored her and pushed her foot into the second boot.

She stood. She took a few steps. She circled the shop. She tapped her feet and then strutted a bit. Then, sitting back down, she took them off and replaced them with the flats. It was like Cinderella sliding into the glass slipper. They were born to fit. They looked so nice. What the hell had she been thinking wearing those other things?

And then, because she was on a roll and it felt great, she walked over to the display and picked up the red stiletto and turned it over. It was her size. She bent down, removed the pump and placed the stiletto on her invisible foot. And then she stood up straight.

"You have great legs," said the sales assistant.

Tilda turned to her. "You think so?"

"I wouldn't say it if I didn't mean it."

Tilda watched her for a moment. She was a pretty little thing, with dark hair pulled back into an elaborate ponytail.

"It must shock you to see my invisible foot."

"Well, I can't *see* it," the girl tittered. "But yeah … it's definitely weird. What happened?"

"I don't know. But I'm trying to fix it."

The girl nodded. "Whenever my mum gets depressed about her age, she goes to Paris."

Tilda stared at the girl. She hadn't said anything about her age, yet the girl had simply assumed it was connected. "Does it make your mum feel better, to go to Paris? What do you think?"

"Doesn't matter what I think. It's what she thinks."

How sweet, thought Tilda, *she looks like a cheerleader but sounds like Yoda.*

She collected all three pairs of shoes and passed them to the girl.

"I'll take them all." Then she handed her the old shoes. "And throw these out. I'll wear the boots."

What happened next was totally out of character for Tilda. First off, instead of returning to work, she continued shopping. She had her new shoes, so was starting from the ground up—with her friend Amanda's help.

The Pantry was quiet, so Amanda could give Tilda her full attention. She was horrified to hear what her friend was going through.

"Oh, darling, what a shit. Let me deck you out. Nothing like a new outfit to make you feel better about things."

Half an hour later, Tilda was handing over her credit card with only the slightest reservation. She had a pair of gray trousers, a black cashmere sweater, a gorgeous white blouse and a black coat. Amanda had insisted she try on an orange shirt, too. It wasn't something she'd normally wear, but seeing as she'd been wearing milking shoes for a couple of years now, that was probably a good thing. She tried it on and was delighted with how she looked. She'd thrown that into the pile, as well as a scarf and a bracelet—and a pair of earrings (even though she only needed one of them).

She decided to ignore the cost. She worked hard. She didn't go over the top. She'd bought herself some long overdue pieces that would mix and match and made her feel fabulous when she was wearing them. Selma would be proud.

Next stop, she stuck her head in at her hairdressers.

"Hello, Tilda. Haven't seen you for a while."

"And it shows. Any appointments today?"

The hairdresser checked the book. "I can fit you in at two."

"Perfect!"

Tilda lugged everything back to the shop, where Debra was loading deliveries into the van.

"Deb, honey, can you run the shop tomorrow?"

"I'd have to delay the deliveries until closing time, but that can work. Why?"

"I've got to go to Paris."

Debra looked worried. "Did someone die?"

"Do I look like the type of person who would only go to Paris in an emergency?"

"Tilly, you never take time off. Well, not until your hand disappeared."

Tilda shook her head in disbelief. Debra was right. It took turning invisible for her to take some time to herself. She looked at her niece, who at twenty-two had style and panache. Deb's daily uniform of cargo pants and zip-up hoodies wasn't Tilda's thing, but it was the way she carried it off, from her bulky boots to her short, spiky hair.

"I need to go to Paris, Deb. Before the rest of me disappears too. I'll leave this afternoon and be back early on Christmas Eve. We're swamped with orders that day."

Debra's face fell. "I know we're busy on Christmas Eve … but I can't work that day."

"Why not?"

"There's something I have to do."

"Can't it wait? We're closed for Christmas and quiet then until New Year."

"It's a bit like your Paris trip, Tilly."

Tilda looked at her niece. Usually she was so tough, but suddenly she looked incredibly vulnerable. She gave her a quick hug. "Okay, I'll manage."

"And I'll manage while you're in Paris. The shop's going to be mine when you cark it anyway." Debra gave Tilda a kiss and marched back outside to the van. "You just go and find yourself."

Find herself? Was it possible to find herself in two nights? And more importantly, was she lost?

Tilda got online and booked a seat on the 16:52 Eurostar to Paris. She pressed 'accept payment', and waited as her ticket was generated. Shit, what had she done?

It doesn't matter what I've done, she thought. *It's what I'm going to do.*

She looked down at her missing hand. She needed this. Or something. She needed something. It was only two nights … one full glorious day. This was her Christmas present to herself. A new wardrobe, a new look, and a day in Paris, her favorite place in the world.

She googled hotels around Notre-Dame. She already knew how she wanted to spend her full day in Paris, and Notre-Dame was a stone's throw away from where it would begin. There were so many hotels to choose from. She flicked through a few. They all looked fine, but she wanted something special.

It took her about ten minutes to find it. The Hotel Antoinette prided itself on its excellent service, spacious rooms, and the *floral artworks* in the hotel restaurant. It was perfect. She booked a room, as well as a table for dinner. Now all she had to do was pack. She'd take her bag to her hair appointment and head straight to the station from there.

And finally, she'd call Patrick. She was putting that off until last. She had to postpone dinner. Patrick answered on the third ring and sounded so pleased to hear from her that Tilda was tempted to cancel her trip. Or to ask him to come with her. But she was also looking forward to a break alone, with no work, just Paris at her feet. Or foot, as the case may be.

"Patrick, I'm afraid I'll have to take a raincheck on dinner tonight."

His voice was filled with disappointment. "Did something come up?"

"I've got some things going on at the moment and—"

"Sure, I understand," he interrupted. "And dating me is just too much to take on right now."

"Oh god, no, Patrick. It's not you. It's me."

"Always is, Tilda."

Tilda almost snapped at him. "Listen, I'm going to Paris because I need some time to think through a personal issue. I'll be back on Christmas Eve, and if you're free, I would love to spend the evening with you."

"You would?"

"Yes, I would."

"So you're not giving me the slip because the whole blind thing has freaked you out?"

"Dating a blind man is the least of my problems, Patrick. In fact, let me rephrase that … It's not a problem. At all."

"Paris, eh?"

"I'll explain when I get home."

"I've got plans to go caroling on Christmas Eve," Patrick said.

A wave of anxiety washed over Tilda. She hadn't been caroling since she was a kid, when a neighbor told her that she was more off key than a lazy locksmith. In fact, she even stopped singing in the shower that day. There's no way she could sing in front of Patrick.

"Don't think about it," Patrick said. "Just say yes."

"Yes."

*

A couple of hours later she was on the Eurostar. She was wearing blue jeans with her new boots and orange shirt, and she'd packed her other new clothes, as well as a lovely dress she'd had for ever but had never worn. Her hair was cut and colored and swinging around her shoulders after a blow-dry. As the train entered the Channel Tunnel, Tilda opened Selma's book.

What if we lived in a world where the young were invisible until they'd earned wisdom? There are many traditional societies around the world where this is the case. Instead, in our more modern society, those with hard-earned wisdom become invisible. They are devalued. It's a frightening prospect, one we remain blissfully unaware of until we hit middle age.

Middle age is a confusing period for anyone. Firstly, we are aware that our currency has waned. It's also that big leap closer to the thing we fear most—death. When middle age arrives, we know about it. It's there. It's in our face ... or on it. Our initial reaction is to reject it. Enter the midlife crisis. There are numerous ways this will play out. Trade in your spouse, subject your body to youth-enhancing treatments. We mourn what has passed without embracing what is. We miss the point completely. Yes, the flush of youth is over ... but in its place should be, could be, true freedom.

It's this freedom that's the key to becoming visible again. Not caring what others think is freeing. Expressing yourself any way you want is freeing. Having opinions, emotional wisdom, spiritual understanding ... these things free you. And in freedom, we find power.

People come to my workshops and I hear the same complaints over and over again: "I'm slowing down. Things don't work like they used to." I say to this, thank god! Yes, there are some dreadful aspects to ageing. But there are also some dreadful aspects to youth. We tend to lose sight of that.

Hands up who wants to go back to the self-doubt, insecurity and blind ignorance of their youth? Age has taught me that what other people think of me is none of my business. I don't care. That lesson alone is worth every wrinkle on my face.

What's the lesson that makes your wrinkles worthwhile? What has the pay-off been for you?

Tilda closed the book, and before she even had time to ponder the question, the answer came to her.

Labels. Oh how she'd struggled with labels. Everyone around her needed to label each other. No one was content to just be. They wanted her to be a dutiful daughter, a good wife, a mother.

Her twenties were all about conforming to these roles. She'd married young, mainly because her parents had encouraged it and she'd spent her whole life trying to please them. Then she'd spent most of her twenties trying to be the perfect wife. God how she'd tried, and failed. She'd divorced Paul, never for a moment thinking that by doing so she was blowing her chance at motherhood. She was young and was sure she'd love again. But it didn't happen. She never did meet "the one" and as a result, her thirties were a struggle, trying not to panic as her biological clock ticked more loudly and took her further and further away from possible parenthood.

It hadn't been easy. She'd poured her love into Debra, and had been the best aunt she could be. But then somewhere around forty, something shifted. She began to accept things. She hadn't just resigned herself to her label-less life—she began to recognize that it was her path and therefore the right path. For whatever reason, she was not, and probably wouldn't be, a wife or a mother. There were people who would never allow that. Even now her parents, her sister, and some of her friends encouraged her to find the one, to marry and have children. At her age IVF was still an option, her mother said. Just.

But Tilda dug her heels in now. People needed to back off. They needed to accept her as she was. To be fair, sometimes she wasn't even sure of who that was, so no wonder her mother was confused. But she knew what she wasn't. She'd worked through it, and it had taken time. It was there on her face. But she'd never trade in that knowledge for a second stab at youth. That much she was sure of.

*

Tilda arrived at the hotel at a little before nine that evening. Her room was lovely, with stone floors, whitewashed walls and wooden beams overhead. There was a large bed with an upholstered headboard and an embroidered cover in rich shades of burgundy. The room was filled with ornate touches like the bronze patina on the light fittings and doorhandles, and gold-framed watercolors. The bathroom was large enough to swing a cat—albeit one with a short tail. All in all, it was perfect.

She opened the window. The sill had a wrought-iron railing that she could lean on and watch Paris below. And she did exactly that. She stuck her head out and looked down at the street, and then across at the twinkling lights of rooms in nearby buildings. She could hear a siren in the distance—a French one. The night air was icy and her breath came out in clouds. As much as the streets of Paris beckoned her, she wouldn't be going out this evening. She'd chosen Hotel Antoinette because she wanted to have dinner downstairs and view the floral art.

Tilda opened her case and hung her clothes in the small closet. Then she laid her dress for dinner out on the bed. She smiled when she saw it, as the memory of how she'd been duped into buying it flooded back.

The local school was holding a fundraiser. The school mothers had offloaded their designer clothes and Debra had pulled this off a rack and shoved it at Tilda.

"Check this out, Aunt Tilly. A brand-new Burberry dress with the label still on it. And it's only £100."

Tilda held the dress. It was lovely. It was black, knee-length, with a V-neck and three-quarter sleeves.

"Do you want it, Deb? My treat."

Debra was busy looking at the Burberry site on her phone. "Holy crap, that dress is selling for £450." She looked up from the phone. "You have to get it."

"Okay, I'll get it for you."

Tilda paid for the dress and afterward found Debra waiting for her nearby.

"Good score, Tilly."

Tilda handed the dress to Debra.

Debra tried not to laugh and handed it straight back. "It's not for me. I thought it would look great on you."

"But I got it for you."

"Tilly, when was the last time you saw me in a dress?"

Something began to dawn on Tilda. "Not for a few years."

Debra nodded. "Because I'm not that sort of lesbian."

"You're a lesbian?"

"That bothers you?" Debra smiled at her aunt.

Tilda laughed and reached out for her niece. "Why would it bother me?" She then drew back and whacked Debra playfully with the shopping bag. "It just means I'm stuck with this dress."

Debra linked her arm through her aunt's. "That the point. You should treat yourself more often."

Tilda slipped the dress on and added some make-up, her new red heels and a black jacket. She looked in the mirror and barely recognized herself. That wasn't true. She recognized herself. And it was the first time in ages.

"I'm taking you out to dinner," she said to her reflection.

The hotel restaurant was lovely. Every detail was utterly perfect. The wallpaper was hand-painted, and the dark wood floors were covered in oriental carpets. A fireplace warmed the room. There was an assorted mix of lounge chairs and divans around small wooden tables. The whole place was an explosion of color, with unusual fabrics and lampshades. And scattered around the restaurant were the reasons she'd chosen the hotel: ten truly stunning flower arrangements. The shades, the form, and the combinations took her breath away.

The restaurant manager greeted her by name and with an appraising stare. "I'm Henri, and am at your service tonight."

At my service? Tilda had to bite back a suggestive remark. Henri was extremely good-looking, if rather formal in both appearance and manner. He took her coat and then led her to a reserved table in the corner.

"Is this suitable?"

Tilda lightly touched the flower arrangement on the bench beside her table. Red tulips, berries and rust-sprayed branches, with some foliage, all in a copper pot.

"This is perfect," Tilda said. "I love the flowers."

"My brother, he does them." Henri said with pride. "He is an artist, no?"

Tilda nodded. "I'm a florist too. In London."

"Ah, another artist." Henri pulled out her chair and then he left her alone with the menu and her thoughts.

Me, an artist? There's a label.

This place is so beautiful.

Will everyone think I'm a total reject because I'm dining alone?

Perhaps if I just casually stare around the room.

Are they kumquats in that arrangement? How clever.

What on earth am I doing in Paris?

I'm in Paris. Oh my god!

By the time the waiter placed her escargots à la bourguignon in front of Tilda, her chattering thoughts had calmed, and so did she. She savored her snails and then the slow-roasted mallard duck and finally the roquefort soufflé with poached pears and walnuts. She relished every bite of the three courses. The robust red from the Rhône region was so good she had a second glass.

She enjoyed dining alone. No one seemed to stare at her like she had a second head (or an invisible nose). Henri appeared occasionally and treated her as though she was an honored guest. Two men seated nearby finished their meal and left the restaurant, but not before one of them gave her an appreciative nod. He could *see* her.

Tilda soaked it all in and thought about what she'd read on the train.

At its very essence, invisibility is an issue with sight. Others can't see you, but that is only the most recent manifestation of this disease. Think back—be honest with yourself.

How do you see yourself?

How do you see others?

And how do you view the world?

Finally, how long have you had this problem with your vision?

Tilda was the first to admit that her view of the world was limited. She was a creature of habit, but those habits didn't include much pleasure.

As Selma had written earlier in the book: *Pleasure is important. With youth, this comes naturally. We're all pleasure seekers. But the years pass, we have more responsibilities, and time becomes the enemy. We don't have time for pleasure. We don't have time.*

Tilda had once found enormous pleasure in her work. It used to be such a joy to design and create flower arrangements. Somewhere along the way, though, it had just become work. That's not to say she was unhappy with her career. She'd never want to do anything else. And she was proud of what she'd accomplished. But her work, along with the rest of her life, had become rather routine. She had a nice apartment, some great friends, and her relationship with Debra. But where was the sparkle? The pleasure? Her only treat was her once-a-month book club—and that was about it. She didn't ever take the initiative to do anything special for herself.

Until now.

Today was special. The hotel, the restaurant, the food. Paris. She was in Paris, in a beautiful dress.

And … she'd been on a date recently. That had also been special.

The irony of Selma's words wasn't lost on her: *Finally, how long have you had this problem with your vision?*

Probably longer than Patrick. He was blind, but his view of the world seemed healthier than hers.

She soaked in the atmosphere. How would Patrick view this place? The fabric on the chair and the tablecloth were rich and felt wonderful under her fingertips. The scent from the flower arrangements was subtle, so as not to overpower the food. The music was faint, but oh so French. She could hear the fire crackling. Chatting in the kitchen.

And suddenly she felt something in her limbs that she hadn't felt for a long time: they felt *present*. Something subsided. She was totally relaxed.

She called Henri over and signed for her meal to be added to her account, then returned to her room. She hung her dress in the closet and slipped into her nightgown. Then she went into the bathroom to wash her face.

As she looked in the mirror she was stunned. She could see her nose again. It was as clear as anything, right there in front of her.

*

Tilda woke early after the best sleep she'd had in ages. She pulled back the curtains and let the morning sun stream in.

Good morning, Paris!

She showered and then dressed in her new trousers and blouse and sweater. She checked herself out in the mirror. She looked nice, but it was her nose that set the whole outfit off. To think she'd always had a problem with it, and wished it was smaller. Looking at it now, it was the loveliest nose she'd ever seen.

Restaurant Antoinette became a buffet breakfast bar in the mornings. She poured herself a coffee and placed two *pains au chocolat* on her plate. She chose another table this morning, next to a display of parrot tulips and miniature roses. She leaned in close to the arrangement to get a better look. Pine needles, eucalyptus pods. What a great choice.

"You like my work?"

Tilda swung around and came face to face with a haughty-looking and very handsome hunk, in dark jeans and a black turtleneck sweater. He gave her the once-over, even her shoes.

"My brother Henri said you are a floral artist from London."

"A florist. Yes. I'm Tilda."

He stuck out his hand. "Alain."

Alain with a capital T for trouble, thought Tilda. It was the middle of a Parisian winter but suddenly the room was hot.

"I chose this hotel because of your flowers," she said.

He looked delighted. "If you are free today, perhaps I can take you to a special place to view some other wonderful foliage."

Christ, there was an offer that was hard to refuse. Hard, yes, but not impossible.

"I'm going to the Marché aux fleurs and the Marmottan Monet museum today. But thank you anyway."

"And this afternoon?"

Tilda looked stumped. She was just planning to get lost in the streets of Paris for a while.

"Do you know Jeff Leatham's work?"

Tilda's eyes widened at the mention the artistic director of the Four Seasons George V. Other women liked movie stars … she had a crush on Europe's top florist. "I know it well, but only from photos."

"How can that be?" Alain asked. "Let me take you to the George V this afternoon. We can view it together."

She'd been so determined to spend time alone. But she also wanted to see the floral arrangements at the George V, especially with someone who was himself a talented florist.

"That would be lovely. Thank you."

He gave her an impossibly sexy smile. "I'll see you back here at four?"

"See you then."

Tilda watched him swagger from the room, and then sat down to breakfast. Meeting Alain had unnerved her a bit, but still she'd do her best to eat both pastries. She bit down on her first *pain au chocolat* and almost moaned out loud. A mouthwatering pastry and a date with a hot man, all before 8 am. It was going to be a glorious day.

But then she thought of Patrick and felt a stab of guilt. She knew it was ridiculous. One date hardly meant she couldn't have some fun here in Paris. And having fun here didn't mean she'd jeopardize whatever it was she had with Patrick.

Tilda finished her coffee and promised herself that she'd stop analyzing everything, and just be in the moment. Starting with the second *pain au chocolat*.

After breakfast, Tilda hit the sidewalk and wandered toward the Marché aux fleurs. She'd discovered this little gem years earlier. It wasn't as impressive as the flower markets the Netherlands had to offer, like Amsterdam's floating Bloemenmarkt or the Aalsmeer Flower Auction, or even the New Covent Garden Market where she bought most of her stock. There were also other markets in Paris she had visited before, but this was the oldest, and with Notre-Dame looming nearby, definitely her favorite.

She entered one of the pavilions and it was a relief to get out of the icy wind blowing off the Seine. The stalls were packed with winter staples of shrubs and trees, hanging baskets and potted plants, but still the place was ablaze with color. She breathed deeply, a symphony of scents greeting her. While spring was no doubt the most spectacular time to visit the market, there were still flowers and plants here that would be unavailable anywhere else.

Tilda lingered by a stall of citrus trees in full bloom. The smell of the blooms and fruits seemed out of place in the Parisian winter. She ran her hand across some of the decorative pots that Parisians used to jazz up their balconies. There were succulents, cacti, violets, pomegranates, hydrangeas, cyclamens, geraniums, bilberries …

She wandered on through the stalls of linens and pottery and knick-knacks. Decorative birdcages and birdhouses swung above her head, waiting for each Sunday, when the Marché aux fleurs became a bird market.

Some stalls were doing a roaring trade in Christmas trees, festive wreaths and decorations. She took her time looking at how the florists had woven the berries and pinecones through the Christmas flower displays.

She bought a small Christmas bell for Patrick. She couldn't help herself. It had such a beautiful sound, it caught her attention and drew her in, and she felt he'd like it. She didn't even know if he had a tree to hang it on ... but if not, he at least had a bell.

She made her way slowly but surely through the market, looking at everything, learning what she could, and allowing the plants to inspire and revitalize her. She was so content to be where she was. She didn't need to rush anywhere, or do anything. She simply was. And she couldn't remember the last time she'd done that. When she eventually emerged into the sun she felt completely reinvigorated.

Next Tilda caught the metro to the sixteenth arrondissement and her favorite Paris museum. The Marmottan Monet museum didn't have the crowds of some of the other more famous museums. Lining up at the Louvre for a glimpse of the *Mona Lisa* had never been Tilda's thing. (Although she had done it—once.) Tilda had always loved Monet, and the Marmottan Monet museum held the largest collection of his work.

She spent a glorious couple of hours looking at pieces by artists like Gauguin, Morisot, Pissarro, Guillaumin, Sisley and Renoir. She wandered through the museum, imagining it to be the grand old home it once was. She claimed the house and its collection of medals and porcelain, furniture, statues and chandeliers as her own. She was having so much fun she was almost shocked whenever she ran into anyone else.

"What are you doing in my home?" she felt like saying.

But it was Monet's work that held her suspended in time, as she moved from his early years right through his life. She stood still before the waterlilies. She lost time in front of *Impression, Sunrise*, the painting from which the Impressionist movement got its name. She finally came out of what felt like a trance. It was nearly three. She needed to get going, to meet Alain. It was with a tinge of regret that she left the Marmottan Monet, promising she'd return much sooner this time.

*

Alain was waiting for her in front of the hotel. His face lit up when he saw her.

"Put this on." He thrust a helmet at her.

Any enthusiasm Tilda had for this adventure suddenly vanished. "We're going on a motorbike?"

"Yes. And that is for your head."

Thank god he clarified that, thought Tilda.

Alain straddled the bike and called over his shoulder. "Get on."

Despite every cell in her body telling her to cancel immediately, Tilda shoved the helmet onto her head and mounted the bike behind Alain. You only live once, and how often did she have the opportunity to press up against a hot Frenchman?

Alain took off and began to zip through traffic at a pace. Tilda squeezed her eyes shut for the first minute or two, praying to various gods, despite being not at all religious. But before long, curiosity and sheer exhilaration got the better of her. She opened her eyes, and without moving too much—she didn't want to fall off—took in the sights around her.

They were flying along the Seine. The wind was in her hair. Or it would've been if it weren't for the helmet. He zoomed around Place de la Concorde and onto the Champs-Élysées. Tilda had gone from being petrified to having the time of her life. She loved the wide streets, the luxury stores, the cafes and restaurants and the beautifully dressed women who strutted past them all. The whole avenue was ablaze with Christmas lights, dripping from the trees.

One final turn down Avenue George V and before long Tilda was peeling herself off the bike and removing her helmet.

Shit, helmet hair. Forgot about that.

Alain took the helmet off her and led her into the hotel. Tilda followed behind, desperately trying to fluff some life back into her hair.

The lobby of the George V was jaw dropping. Tilda felt like she'd died and gone to heaven.

"I come here for inspiration," said Alain. "Every week twelve thousand flowers are brought here from Amsterdam."

"It's unbelievable, Alain."

"Over the holiday season they don't use as many flowers, so they add the extra decorative things like lights and candles."

"Are they just in the lobby?"

"There are nearly two hundred displays all over the hotel. But the main public areas have the major displays." Alain waved his hand around. "Every three weeks, Jeff Leatham and his team develop a floral theme for the hotel. We can see this one is influenced by Christmas."

Tilda looked around. Not only were there a number of spectacular floral arrangements, but there were also a few huge sculptures and installations made out of lights. Alain led her over to the window where she could see more lit trees in a courtyard.

"This is possibly the most beautiful place I've ever seen," Tilda sighed.

Alain looked at her. "Let's have a drink."

He grabbed her hand and led her through the foyer. Tilda didn't argue ... with him, but internally she went to war with herself.

What the hell was she doing? He was nice, and extremely hot, but she wasn't interested. At all. He was much younger than her. Her money was on mid to late thirties. And as much as her friends joked about the whole cougar thing, it didn't appeal to her.

But mainly … there was Patrick.

When she'd climbed onto Alain's motorbike, her first thought had been, "I bet Patrick would like this."

She'd flown down the Champs-Élysées and thought, "What would this be like for Patrick?"

She'd walked into the George V and wished he was with her. Not this sexy Frenchman. That wasn't true. Alain was very knowledgeable about the hotel and flowers, so he could come too. But Tilda would be with Patrick.

She wanted to be.

Instead, it was Alain who led her into the bar and pulled up a stool and opened a cocktail menu. He leaned over and she pretended to read it with him, but mostly she just wanted him to get out of her personal space.

"How about a Quick Farewell?" he said.

"Sounds good to me." And it did.

"Or a Bye Bye Baby Goodbye?"

"That's perfect. I want that one."

"Okay, you have that and I will get a Loving You All Night."

Alain ordered the cocktails and then twisted his stool around and perused the room. "It's beautiful here, no?"

"No. I mean yes." She relaxed a little. How could she not enjoy being here? She soaked in the surroundings. The wood paneling, the red velvet chairs and candle chandelier. It was a beautiful room.

"Oh my god," hissed Alain.

Tilda drew back. What had she done? Suddenly Alain's hand clutched at her knee.

"Oh my god!"

Alain looked like he was going to hyperventilate. Was he having some sort of attack? Tilda followed his gaze to a table in the corner, where two men and a woman sat. And then she saw that one of the men was Jeff Leatham.

"Is it him?" she whispered.

"Yeeeeeeees," said Alain through clenched teeth.

And it was right at that moment that the penny dropped. Alain was gay. How she'd missed it was beyond her. Although, there had been nothing to indicate that he was gay before this moment. There was nothing to indicate that he was straight, either. She'd jumped to a conclusion about his sexuality simply because he'd been kind to her. His offer to bring her here, to share this with her, was because he figured she'd appreciate the beauty of the place. It was more a moment from *When Two Florists Meet* than anything romantic.

She was simultaneously a little let down and completely relieved. She grabbed Alain's hand and gave it a squeeze as the party of three stood and walked out of the bar.

"He's taller than I expected," Tilda whispered.

Alain clutched her hand until they'd disappeared. And then, the two of them turned to each other and began to laugh.

"No one but you would understand," he said.

"He's like a rock star to our kind."

"We flower people," he whispered.

"Foliage freaks," Tilda teased.

They roared with laughter, aware that they'd just shared something special. The drinks arrived and they toasted each other.

"Thank you for sharing this with me, Alain."

"I knew you would appreciate it."

"Here's to appreciating it."

And they drank to that, and then to numerous other things as well.

"So, tell me about your love-life." Alain leaned right over to her as though things were going to get interesting.

"Sorry to disappoint, but I don't have one."

"None?" He clearly thought she was lying. "You are so lovely."

Tilda was taken aback. "I haven't felt lovely for a long time. I've felt … old."

"We say in French, *si la jeunesse est la plus belle des fleurs, la vieillesse est le plus savoureux des fruits*."

"Something about fruit?"

"If youth is the most beautiful of flowers, old age is the tastiest fruit. You are not old, Tilda, but when you are, you will be … a mango!"

Tilda could barely control her laughter. "I'm so glad I met you, Alain."

"Let me think, do I know any single straight men?" Alain pretended to put on his thinking cap.

"That's not necessary. While I don't officially have a boy-friend … I did meet someone recently."

"I knew it. He's handsome, no?"

"Yes, very. His name is Patrick."

"Patrick. I like this name. Tell me about *Patrick*." He gave Patrick's name a French flair.

Tilda found she wanted to talk about him. "He's tall. Very tall. And kind of scruffy, but in a very sexy way. I don't mean his clothes. They're always immaculate. But he often has a three-day growth, and his hair has this messy wave in it."

It was only at this point that Tilda remembered Patrick was also blind. It amazed her to think that she had this image of him, and was describing it, but that the blindness wasn't part of that. Was it possible, for her to be with him and for the blindness to not be an issue? She didn't know, but she wanted to find out.

"He sounds perfect."

"He's amazing, but there would be challenges as well," Tilda said.

"There are with every relationship."

"Patrick is blind."

"In his eyes?"

"Yes."

"In his heart?"

"Not at all."

Alain gave a shrug, like it was no problem. "Then he'll still see you."

"You know, he does. He absolutely does."

"Does he have a dog?"

"No, he uses a cane."

"Then it's all good." Alain smiled cheekily. "I know I'm French, but I fucking hate dogs."

*

The ride back to the hotel was even nicer. It was dark, so Paris was lit up like fairyland. Alain took a detour past the Eiffel Tower and it was just magic. Tilda was way more relaxed on the bike, and certainly happy to hold Alain tight. They were friends now.

They gave each other a huge hug outside Hotel Antoinette and he promised to come and visit her in London. And then, off he zipped into the night.

Tilda heard her phone ringing. She shuffled around her bag, but by the time she found her phone it had stopped. Three missed calls. One from Eva, one from Paige. And one from Patrick. She quickly called him back and he answered on the first ring.

"Tilda!"

"Hi, Patrick—I missed your call."

"What a coincidence. I missed you."

Tilda laughed. "I missed your call ... and I missed you too."

"You have? That's good news. I didn't want to be sad stalker Patrick."

"Never."

"So how's Paris?"

Tilda looked up at the city around her. "Glorious. I can see Notre-Dame from where I'm standing."

"Describe it for me."

So Tilda did. And she walked the streets of Paris for the next two hours, taking Patrick on a tour.

*

The shop had been hectic all day, with last-minute Christmas arrangements. Tilda had enjoyed every minute of it. She felt like her designs were more interesting than anything she'd done in years. Certainly her customers were pleased. The only thing that marred her day was a call from Eva in Vienna, giving her some news about Paige, but she was yet to speak to her friend, whose phone was off.

Tilda closed for lunch and did all the deliveries that Debra would normally do. She texted Debra: *Happy Christmas Eve, my love. All good here. Enjoy wherever you are.* She also used the opportunity to call Selma. It was an emergency number, but Selma had assured her that she didn't mind her using it. The phone rang and rang, but then just as Tilda was about to hang up, Selma answered, sounding out of breath.

"Sorry to bother you, Selma. It's Tilda—"

More panting. "Yes, dear. Everything all right?"

"I'm not sure if this is an emergency, but I need some advice."

Tilda could hear a muffled voice in the background and what sounded like a slap.

"Is this a bad time to call, Selma?"

"Not at all. I just finished with my personal trainer. Zumba! Nearly kills me."

"Oh ... I can call back."

"Hell, no. I'm about to have a massage. Now's good."

Tilda decided to be quick. "I was in Paris and my nose came back."

Selma didn't sound at all surprised. "Paris will do that to you."

"Then I was reading your book on the Eurostar and noticed that my foot is visible again. The hand and ear are still a little fuzzy, but the rest of me is as clear as day."

"Whatever you're doing, keep it up."

"Does it mean I'll be cured?"

"It's up to you." There was a strange noise, and then Selma continued. "Come and see me in the new year. We'll keep working on it. But it sounds like you're well on your way."

"Thank you, Selma. And merry Christmas."

"I'm Jewish. But thanks anyway, dear."

And with that, Selma hung up. Tilda glanced at her phone. She had the most glorious feeling of butterflies in her tummy. She had to get back to the shop, finish up the last of the Christmas orders, deliver them, and then she could close shop and meet Patrick. She'd have to explain to him that she couldn't sing, but it was hardly a deal-breaker. Instead of feeling stressed, she felt grateful that life was so good.

*

"Patrick!"

Patrick's face lit up when he heard Tilda's voice. She ran up to him, and without thinking, gave him a kiss.

"Merry Christmas."

"It's merry now," Patrick said. "Ready for some caroling?"

"As ready as I'll ever be," Tilda said.

They walked through the backstreets of Muswell Hill together.

"What's that you're carrying?"

"It's my viola."

"Oh great, I'll hear you play." Then the moment of truth. "I'm not much of a singer, Patrick."

"I'm not much of a cook."

Tilda shook her head. He could be so silly, but she liked it. "Perhaps, but we're going caroling tonight, not cooking."

"I was going to ask you back to my place for dinner afterward."

"Okay, I'd like that."

"As long as you don't make fun of my cooking skills." He reached out and squeezed her hand. "And I'll try to not make fun of your singing."

"I could just hum."

"Or dance. Whatever makes you happy, Tilda."

As it turned out, the caroling group was a large group of people from the neighborhood where Patrick's grandmother lived. There were older people, parents and their kids, a few young couples. Everyone seemed to know Patrick and enthusiastically embraced Tilda into the group. It had been a local tradition for years to carol on the doorsteps of the elderly neighbors.

"Patrick!" a woman called across the crowd.

Patrick turned toward the voice. "That's my sister, Misha."

Misha moved through the crowd toward them. She was tall and attractive, like Patrick, and leading an elderly woman who was also blind and using a cane.

"You didn't tell me I'd be meeting your family," Tilda hissed.

"You're not. Only Misha and my grandmother." Then Patrick called out, "Gran, you've got to meet a friend of mine."

Misha led her grandmother right up to Patrick. "Where's my boy?" the older woman said.

Patrick reached out and gave his grandmother a hug. Then he took her hand and one of Tilda's and placed them together. "Gran, this is Tilda."

"The girl with the flower shop?"

Tilda was surprised Patrick had told his grandmother about her. "Yes, and I loved your orchids."

"Then you'll have to come and see where I keep them." She gave Tilda a hug. "Call me Peg."

"And I'm Misha." Patrick's sister shook her hand enthusiastically. "It's nice to meet you."

The group set up camp at the end of the quiet street. A few of the neighbors had made pots of gluhwein and everyone drank up. A number of people had brought instruments along.

They started with "Good King Wenceslas". Patrick had a great voice, and Tilda loved watching him play the viola. He didn't use sheet music, but then none of the musicians did. They just seemed to know how to jam together.

Tilda started singing softly but Patrick poked her in the ribs a few times, which got her laughing and singing louder. Next up was "The First Noel", then "The Twelve Days of Christmas", which Tilda just swayed to because she only knew three of the twelve days.

She watched the crowd, everyone laughing and embracing this wonderful Christmas tradition that she hadn't even thought about for decades. But mainly, she watched Patrick, and something inside her started to shift. Here was a man who had been dealt a hand of cards that many people would toss in. But he played that hand. He was so engaged with the people around him. He embraced life.

Tilda wanted to know him better. She wanted to talk and never stop talking to him. She wanted to know if he saw images when he dreamed, and if he was ever afraid of the dark. She wanted to hear about his childhood and his dreams for the future. What was his favorite color? Did he remember colors well? What tea did he drink? What moved him to tears?

She wanted to reach out and touch his face, because it was so beautiful. She wanted to know what it was like to wake up with him. And she wanted to know what it was like to lie naked with him.

And she would. Of that she was sure. She could envision that. She saw everything clearly now.

She moved closer to him. He placed a hand on her face and then leaned forward and kissed her forehead. Then he put the viola back under his chin and belted out "Joy to the World."

And Tilda joined in, at the top of her lungs.

Clementine

Christmas Eve

Clementine's knees were shaking. What was she doing? Seriously! Turning up here unannounced like this *was* crazy.

She entered Sam's apartment block and walked up the three flights of stairs. Each step of the way, she looked for an excuse to run. A sign that this was the wrong thing to do. But the stairwell was quite lovely. It was neat. Some of the apartments had potted plants outside the door, and welcome mats, which made Clementine feel better.

She reached Sam's door and took a few deep breaths to calm herself.

It didn't work.

She could hear music inside and pressed her ear to the door. Perhaps she should call first. Not that she had Sam's phone number. Just Skype.

Bugger it. She was here. And she looked hot, in her boots and jeans. Her fringe was swept to one side. She was wearing cute cat-eye glasses. She'd had second thoughts about her jacket. Debra had taken one look at this one and laughed.

"You look like you work for FedEx."

"That's not nice, Debra. It makes me feel like shit."

"Bollocks. I always tell you when you look hot."

That was true. She was a good friend like that.

Clementine looked down at her coat. It was just a jacket. She'd remove it immediately anyway. Time to do it. She knocked.

God, she was so nervous. She clutched Sam's present in front of her.

She heard the lock. The door swung open, and … it was a pretty blonde woman about her own age.

"Hi, do I need to sign for that?"

Clementine was thrown. Her eyes darted past the blonde to another woman, with dark hair and a familiar face, walking down the hall.

"Who is it, honey?"

"Delivery."

"I'll sign for it," she said to the blonde.

The blonde turned and gave her a kiss. "Aren't you sneaky, Sammy. Another present for me."

And with that she disappeared down the hall.

"Clementine?"

"Your back healed quickly."

"I thought you understood," said Samantha. "I live with someone."

"I thought you meant a roommate."

Sam's blue eyes flashed angrily. "Are you seriously that naive?"

And with that, Clementine turned and fled from the building.

Sadie

Christmas Day

Sadie ignored the throbbing in her skull that warned her not to open her eyes, ever, ever again, and did so anyway. Big mistake. He was there. He was next to her and looked nothing like the guy she'd come home with. That guy had been sexy, and charismatic, with an aristocratic air about him. This snoring beast had probably killed that guy, stowed the body and crawled into Sadie's bed while she slept.

Fuck vodka, fuck lime, fuck soda, and fuck why did she drink so much?

Christmas, that's why.

Sadie tried to pull her arm out from under him, but it was stuck. She considered chewing it off, but didn't want the blood to ruin her new sheets ... although letting Yeti-man shag her in them had pretty much destroyed her fondness for them anyway. Amazing how you could have three (okay, twelve) drinks too many and think that you're christening a new set of sheets, when you're just creating cringe-worthy memories you'll relive every time you hang them on the line.

Why oh why oh why did she shag him? They'd had such a nice night. He was a nice guy. But he wasn't her type. She *totally* wasn't attracted to him. And she hated to think that by shagging him she'd given him the impression that she was.

He stirred slightly, and, bless him ... quietly farted. Either that or he was lying on a mouse. Sadie couldn't remember reading about that little idiosyncrasy on his VIP profile. It had assured her that he loved exploring new places (okay, so she could vouch for that), eating out (once again ...), and was a voracious reader (he sure as hell kept reading the drinks menu last night!). But in all honesty, it was the quote. Sadie was a sucker for a good quote and Yeti-man here—or BookBoy55—had quoted Eleanor Roosevelt: "Great minds discuss ideas. Average minds discuss events. Small minds discuss people."

What chance did she have? She didn't care if he'd got the quote from a Celestial Seasonings tea packet. As a full-time single mother she was so sick of discussing school events and who did what to whom in the playground. She desperately missed discussing ideas. The only time anything of any real meaning came out her mouth was when she was at her monthly book club. The rest of the time it was just "pick that up" and "don't hit your sister/brother" and "eat your vegetables." She was desperate for some adult conversation. Some adult connection. She wanted to talk to someone. So she'd agreed to go out with BookBoy55 hoping they would be able to talk.

And they did. He was smart and funny and it was the best evening of conversation she'd ever had. The problem was his looks. He wasn't her type. She liked pretty boys. Her friend Amanda had recently joked that she liked them young, dumb and full of cum. And she certainly had a history with that type of guy. But Sadie was the first to admit she was looking for something *a little* different now. She wasn't interested in dumb … just young and cum.

Sadie wanted young, hot and smart. Was it too much to ask? Apparently, yes. This one was smart. But he also looked like the abominable snowman. He was huge. Tall, stocky, with big hands and features. Big everything, she now knew … She lay there staring at the ceiling, holding her aching head with her free hand. Why oh why oh why did she shag him? She scoured her brain for where things went off track. What the hell had happened last night?

*

Sadie walked into the restaurant and looked around. A large man in the corner was waving at the waiter, or waving away flies, but she couldn't see her date. Damn it. She'd made sure she was late. She was nervous enough without arriving before her date. She was just about to ask to be seated when the waving giant stood and made his way toward her. She looked around. Was he coming to greet someone behind her? No. She realized with a sinking heart that this was BookBoy55. And by the time he reached her, large hand outstretched, big smile on his face, she was wondering how she was going to get out of the date.

"Sadie, Harry. You look just like your photo."

"Nice to meet you." *You look nothing like yours*, she thought.

Sadie silently fumed as she followed him back to the table. The photo he'd posted on the dating site was at least twenty years out of date. He must be twenty years older than her, and looked it, with his graying hair and beard. He looked more like Hagrid from Harry Potter than her ideal man. What a complete waste of time. She'd rather be home with a book.

He pulled her chair out for her and waited until she was seated to return to his own. He sat back and watched her for a moment. He didn't seem nervous. In fact, he came across as a man very comfortable in his own skin. But then, thought Sadie, he'd had years to get used to it.

He opened the drinks menus and placed it in front of her. "Do you like wine? The Journey Valley cab sav is particularly good here."

"I'll have a vodka lime and soda." She didn't mean to snap, but did.

He didn't react. "Excellent. I think I'll join you." He called the waiter over. "Four vodka lime and sodas, thank you."

Sadie raised an eyebrow. "Four?"

"Yes, I figure we can slam one back and sit on the second. Might break the ice."

Sadie smiled, for the first time since she'd arrived. "I've never done this before."

"Order four vodkas?"

"No, I've done plenty of that."

"Then you must mean the online dating thing."

"Yes. I'm way out of my comfort zone."

"I find that's the best place to start." Harry smiled. "So I know that you're thirty-six, Libran, with two young kids and an interest in sports and an unquenchable thirst for reading."

"You memorized my profile."

"It wasn't that long."

"Well, it sums me up."

"Oh, I highly doubt that. Even the most average people can't be summed up in one sentence." He watched her across the table. "Tell me about this unquenchable thirst."

Sadie shuffled in her seat. Unquenchable thirst? Where the hell were the drinks? "It was probably a daft way to describe how I feel. To be honest, I've only become an avid reader in the past couple of years. Since having kids and especially since my divorce."

"Books are great company."

"So I've discovered." Certainly better company than her ex, Craig, who wasn't the brightest bulb in the box. Unfortunately he was a good-looking one, and it had taken Sadie seven years to recognize that beneath the drop-dead gorgeous exterior lay ... well, not much.

The drinks arrived and they paused to order their meal. Then they smiled across the table at each other, clinked their first drinks, and tossed them back. Sadie felt the vodka hit her immediately. She picked up her second drink and sipped it slowly through a straw.

"Your profile said you're an archaeologist." It was that that had caught Sadie's eye, not his out-of-date photo. She'd also missed all the other details on the profile. She'd just read *archaeologist* and knew she wanted to meet him.

"I'm a rescue archaeologist for the British Museum."

"What does that mean?"

"Let's say a developer goes into an area and starts tearing it up and comes across a find. They don't want to waste time and money allowing the place to be excavated. So people like me fly in and we do our best to save, move, and preserve the archaeological site or monument."

Sadie was genuinely impressed. "You're like a superhero for artifacts."

"I even have a cape and tights," Harry grinned.

Sadie ran her eyes over his chest. He was a big man, that's for sure. Pity about the lazy eye. It wasn't too noticeable. Most people wouldn't be aware of it at all. But Sadie could pick everything from a scurfy scalp to a stray nasal hair a mile away. She didn't mean to notice people's faults. They just jumped out at her.

She sipped her vodka. "So your profile said you're divorced with kids?"

"Two sons and a daughter, all adults now."

"Why did you get divorced?"

"We'd outgrown each other. It takes some courage to admit it and fortunately my ex-wife is a courageous woman. We've remained friends."

"Do you see her often?"

"We have dinner when she's in London. She's French and lives in Paris now. She's a lecturer at the Sorbonne."

Sadie suddenly felt embarrassed by her "I'm an avid reader" speech. Harry seemed to sense that and changed the subject.

"How about you, Sadie? What do you do?"

The second vodka was hitting the spot and she motioned for the waiter to bring some more. "What do I do? Not much, Harry." Sadie laughed, but there was a bitter thread beneath it. "I met my ex, Craig, when I was twenty. I was a fitness instructor at the gym he owned. I helped him build up his business. We opened a second, and then a third. By the time we divorced he had eight gyms all over London. Have you heard of Munn's Gyms?"

Harry looked apologetic. "I'm not much of a gym person, sorry, Sadie."

"No need to apologize. Turns out nor am I." Sadie leaned forward on the table. "Around the time I had the kids, it finally occurred to me that I was bored out of my brain. I was still doing the books. I dealt with the accountants. Craig was more the frontman, I ran the back end. I stopped going to the gym, as you can probably tell."

"No, I can't. I think you're stunning."

Sadie was taken aback. She couldn't remember the last time a man had been so straightforward about her attractiveness.

The fact that she'd stopped working out had been a huge bone of contention between her and Craig.

Sadie looked around the room, unsure what she was trying to say. Then, because she felt she had nothing to lose with this man, she said, "I agreed to come out tonight because your profile sounded interesting. And quite frankly, my life has been rather dull for some time."

"Then give me a chance to interest you."

"I thought I was."

"You've had one eye on the door since you arrived. How about you slip your shoes off and relax. It's one night out of your life. Take this night and see if I interest you."

Sadie stared at him. He was already interesting. He just wasn't attractive. That wasn't true either. He was striking, and certainly had a powerful build. She felt like she was dining with a Viking. But she'd be lying if she said he was her type.

Although her type was up for review.

Sadie had been so bowled over by Craig's looks that she hadn't noticed he lacked substance. Since the divorce, she'd only slept with one man. He was younger than her, and prettier, which they both silently acknowledged when they woke up together. It's why she'd changed the age range on her VIP online dating profile. She couldn't bear the humiliation again—or the thought of another evening of mundane conversation that eventually led to less than average sex. She hadn't even had an orgasm.

Sadie smiled at Harry and slipped her shoes off.

"Great. Now … let's get to know each other."

And they did. They talked over their meal, and a few more vodkas. Then they went to a nearby bar and kept drinking. He held open doors, guided her across roads, pulled out chairs. He paid for dinner, and paid her compliments.

And best of all, he was interested in what she had to say.

"I've been looking after my friend's bookshop for the past few days while she's dealing with some personal stuff."

"Are you enjoying it?"

"I love it." Sadie's eyes lit up. "It's called the Happy Endings bookshop."

"I know it. In Muswell Hill. Lovely little shop." He smiled at her. "Are you after a happy ending?"

Sadie was embarrassed. "Aren't we all? But what does it mean, anyway? I'd rather have a happy beginning and work up from there."

"True. Not much point of a happy ending. What do you think being happy means?"

Christ, when was the last time a man had asked her opinion on anything? "I think people waste a lot of time thinking, *if I had that person, that job, that house, that body ... then I'd be happy*. I think it's about a shift in perspective. It's seeing things clearly."

"Do you see things clearly?"

"Not always. I've spent most of my life being bloody superficial."

They stared at each other for a moment and she had a sudden and surprising surge of attraction toward him. He knew it too. He reached out and took her hand, and then continued talking. It felt like the most natural thing in the world.

They talked about books, and films and politics. He shared funny stories from the field about finding mummified remains and ancient civilizations. Harry had traveled far and wide, and listened to her dreams of how she wanted to. And as each hour passed, with each drink consumed, he became more and more attractive.

Until he led her into a taxi and home to her new sheets.

"You are one fucking gorgeous creature," Harry growled as he peeled off her clothes the minute they got in the front door.

She could get used to these compliments.

Before she knew it, she was standing in nothing but her underwear in the hallway.

Harry pushed her against the wall and kissed her. Christ, he could kiss. He was good at it too.

"You taste delicious." One hand skillfully undid her bra at the back while the other grabbed hold of her breast and lifted it to his lips. He ran his tongue over her nipple. She wrapped her arms around him. He was so big, so fucking masculine.

Her hand ran across his jeans and she felt something straining to get out.

"Let me touch you," she groaned.

"Not yet." His hand slipped into her underwear and then deftly parted her lips. And then one finger, just one finger, slowly rubbed—barely touching, it was so gentle.

"Feel how wet you are, Sadie?"

"Yes."

"That means you want me."

"I do."

Sadie was still standing, pressed against the wall, but it was only his free arm holding her upright. Her legs were weak beneath her. She felt like she was dissolving.

He parted her legs and kneeled before her. His hands wrapped around her waist while his mouth ran a trail across her stomach ... and down ... inside her thigh ... until his tongue gently rested on her, and then as she began to quiver beneath it, he began to lick.

"Oh god, Harry."

And lick.

"Oh god."

And lick. His hands grabbed her arse, clutching her cheeks, and lifting her up so he could lick and lick until she screamed and grabbed hold of his hair.

"Oh my ... ohhhhh ..."

And just as she came, he thrust his tongue deep inside her, as she pulsated around it.

He lifted her into his arms as her legs melted beneath her. "Where's your bedroom?"

"End of the hall," she purred.

He strode into her room, tossed her on the bed and tore his own clothes off. Sadie's eyes widened when she saw his cock.

He moved on top of her, eyes locked. 'I've wanted to be inside you from the moment you walked into that restaurant."

And with that he was.

And it was so fucking good. He devoured her, mentally, physically. And she wanted him, how she wanted him. She wanted to fuck his mind, his soul ... not to mention that massive cock.

The third time she came, she cried. He was, bar none, the most amazing lover she'd ever had.

Which goes to show what a weird sense of humor God has, because she simply wasn't attracted to him. She wasn't.

Oh god, why did she sleep with him? Yes, she'd been horny. She hadn't been laid for ages. She certainly hadn't expected to get laid last night, though, especially once she laid eyes on him. But it was Christmas Eve. She still wasn't used to spending Christmas Eve alone while the kids were with Craig. And the cocktails had made him more attractive.

Drink till he's cute. That had been her motto last night.

Because there was no way she was actually attracted to him.

She glanced at the clock: 9:10 am. She needed to get moving. Craig would be dropping the kids back at ten. Having her one-night stand greet the kids at the door on Christmas morning would never win her mother of the year. But more importantly (which once again illustrated what a dreadful mother she was), she didn't want Craig to see him.

Craig, who'd been the most stunning man Sadie had ever met.

Craig, who still turned heads everywhere he went.

Craig ... who only ever dated women who looked like they'd just stepped out of a magazine.

Yes, she'd had her moment of glory herself, but that moment was over the instant she tore her perineum during childbirth. Craig had never again looked at her the same way. From that moment on, she was flawed. She simply couldn't let Craig see that she'd shagged someone like Harry. It was embarrassing. He had to go.

She tapped his shoulder. "Ah ... 'scuse me ... morning."

"Hmphrumpole ..."

How charming ... he could speak in tongues. And then Sadie remembered she already knew that factoid. He was quite a cunning linguist.

There was that molten heat again.

She pushed him a bit harder. "Hey ... wake up."

He stirred.

Finally one lazy eye opened after another ... well, one opened ... the lazy one just lolled there. Last night Sadie had found it quirky, but in the harsh light of day it was downright disturbing.

"Morning," he grinned.

"You have to go," she said.

He reached for her, but she dodged his embrace and slipped out of bed. "My ex is dropping the kids home."

"Would you like me to meet them now?" he asked.

Now? As opposed to ... never, thought Sadie. "Some other time." *June 2087.*

"Sure, no hurry."

He stretched and then lumbered out of bed. He was enormous. Beside him Sadie felt tiny. She forgot about the extra weight that had been bothering her for months. She felt like a little twig of a thing. And she liked that.

He stepped into his boxer shorts as she watched. He wasn't fat at all. Maybe an extra pound or two, but most of his body was solid. She imagined he'd been quite a looker when he was younger, and then silently berated herself. She had been too. But his arms were big, and his chest endless, in a rugged, cave man kind of way.

He noticed her watching and smiled. "I had fun last night, Sadie."

She blushed. "Yes … it was lovely to meet you and hear all about your work." What a ridiculous thing to say in her underwear. Next she'd be asking if they could be penpals.

But she did enjoy hearing about his work. She enjoyed every word he uttered. Suddenly she felt so out of her depth. She was awash with feelings she didn't understand and didn't like. She felt completely vulnerable. She wanted him to leave.

He seemed to sense her confusion, and before she could stop him, he drew her into his arms for a hug. She froze.

"Merry Christmas."

"Yes, you too." *Okay, let me go now.*

He held her tight. She responded like limp lettuce.

He didn't let go. She sensed he was like that about a lot of things.

And then, against her better judgement, she began to relax. She hugged him back. So he wasn't Hugh Jackman, but he was a nice guy. Perhaps they could be friends. She knew he was alone for Christmas. He told her that he saw his family on Boxing Day. She wrapped her arms as far around his big frame as she could, and held him tight. How good it felt. She couldn't remember the last time a man had held her like he cared. She breathed in his scent. It was strong and yet familiar. It stirred something deep inside her. His embrace did something that she thought impossible—it made everything okay.

She pulled away, her mind a jumble of conflicting thoughts. They stared at each other. There was a moment of pure heat between them and she suddenly needed him inside her. *Needed* him, like she'd never needed anyone before. And then … the doorbell rang. She could hear laughter, and her daughter calling out, "Merry Christmas, Mummy."

"Oh shit, my kids. They're early."

Sadie grabbed her jeans and shimmied into them. "Oh shit, no, this is not good."

"It's okay, don't freak out. I'm a friend who dropped by for Christmas breakfast. All good."

She paused, looked at him. He was calm. He was right. "Good idea."

Sadie threw on her shirt, tied her hair back in an elastic band, and raced out of her room and toward the front door. "Bugger, bugger, bum." She raced back and found Harry, now fully dressed. "Wait in the lounge," she told him, "it's just down the hall." Then she raced for the front door again.

And then she opened it, and standing there were her reasons for breathing. Stella, six, Max, five … faces alight with Christmas excitement. She threw her arms around them.

"Merry Christmas, my munchkins."

"Look, we got iPads!" squealed Stella.

Sadie pasted a fake smile on her face. More inappropriate gifts from their dad. "That's great. How about you run inside and look under the tree? And I've got a friend in there who's having breakfast with us, so don't get a fright."

The kids disappeared and Sadie looked at Craig.

"A friend?" he said, a sneer on his face. "What sort of friend, Sadie?"

She said nothing. He'd lost the right to an explanation the moment he shagged Michelle from the gym.

"Merry Christmas, Craig." And with that she closed the door on him. Yes, she'd had the last word. Damn that felt good. She put her eye to the peephole. He was still standing there, one finger raised at her. Bugger, he knew her too well.

She could hear the kids talking in the lounge room. And then a deeper voice, followed by the three of them laughing. She quickly made her way toward them and then paused at the door.

"Are you sure you're not Santa? You look like him."

"No, I'm not Santa."

"But you have the same beard," said Stella.

"And kind eyes," said Max.

Sadie almost fell over. Kind eyes? What a bizarre thing for him to say.

"I really, really, really think you're Santa," said Max.

"I hope you are," Stella giggled.

"Hmmm ... well, I'm not. But I do know Santa."

"YOU DO?"

"Yes, he's my second cousin, on my father's side. That's why there's the resemblance."

"I knew it!" Max said.

"You're a very cluey kid."

"What's Santa like?"

"He's nice. I occasionally see him at family get-togethers. But he's very busy, especially leading up to Easter."

Max and Stella thought that was hilarious. "Not Easter! Christmas."

Yeti-man slapped his forehead. "You're right, I meant Christmas."

Sadie entered the room. "So you've met my friend Hagrid."

"Er ... Harry."

"I mean Harry." *Shit, shit.*

"Mummy, Harry is Santa's cousin."

"I know. I heard." Sadie smiled.

Harry stood, dwarfing the Christmas tree. "Anyway, I'd better be off and let you guys open your presents." He gave the kids a wink. "Let me know if you're not happy with them and I'll email my cousin."

"You said he was here for breakfast," Stella whined.

Sadie looked at him. Max was right. He had such kind eyes. "Why don't you stay for breakfast?"

Harry smiled. "Are you sure?"

Sadie almost fell over as Stella slipped her hand into Harry's. "Please stay for breakfast."

Sadie looked at her children as a wave of shame engulfed her. They saw magic in this man. She'd been so caught up in the superficial things that she'd missed it. Almost.

"I'd love you to stay," she said. And she meant it.

Clementine

Christmas Eve

Stupid, stupid, she was so stupid. She'd spent months falling for Samantha's lies. She'd spent money she didn't have coming over here. She'd ignored the warnings from people who cared about her: Paige, her parents, Sadie and Amanda. And Debra. God, she'd been so dismissive of Debra, when she'd been right all along.

And now she was all alone for Christmas in a city she already despised.

Clementine sobbed all the way back to the hotel. As soon as she was in her room, she threw herself on the bed. What she'd give to be at home now, with Deb, watching movies and eating one of her seriously delicious cheesecakes.

She blew her nose and scrounged through her bag for her phone. She checked her phone and saw three messages from Deb.

So what's happening? Have you met Sam?

Then an hour later:

Can you give me an update so I know you're okay?

Another twenty-seven minutes later.

Just fucking let me know you're not in a ditch somewhere!

Clementine laughed through her tears. Debra came across as so tough but she was like a mother hen. She messaged her back.

I'm okay. I'm in my hotel room.

Debra's response pinged back almost immediately.

Thank god. I was getting worried. So are you with Sam?

It was killing Clementine to admit it, but if she couldn't talk to Debra about it, then who could she talk to?

I messed up, Deb. She was horrible. She lives with someone.

Clementine waited for Debra's reply. It was bound to be funny. She waited. And waited. Nothing, so she messaged her again.

Deb, did you get my last message?

No answer.

No doubt you're rolling around the floor laughing. Or getting your "I told you so" speech ready.

There was a knock on the door. Clementine walked over to answer it, glancing at the screen of her phone as she did, willing Debra to answer. She swung the door open and …

"I wasn't getting my 'I told you so' speech ready. I was legging it up from the hotel cafe, where I've been sitting for the past three hours."

"Deb!" And Clementine burst into tears. "What the hell?"

Debra wrapped her arms around Clementine. "I couldn't let you spend Christmas alone."

Clementine melted into the embrace. It was exactly where she wanted to be. What had she been thinking? She pulled back and looked at the woman who had been her best friend for over two years.

"Jesus Christ, Deb. How did I miss it?"

Debra gently pushed a locked of hair back from Clementine's face. "Selective vision, Clem. Sometimes it takes a while to see what's right in front of us."

Paige

The universe is full of magical things patiently waiting for our wits to grow sharper.
                                    Eden Phillpotts

Two days before Christmas

Paige stood in front of the quirky-looking cottage and
wondered what the hell had come over her. What would
possess a woman of her age to take off into the countryside
with three witches and her mother's physiotherapist?

"You okay, Paige?" Arley seemed to read her mind.

"No ... I don't think I am."

"Nothing like a good shake-up of one's world to get things
in perspective," said Arley.

Paige didn't respond.

"Go on in, you guys," called Calypso as she unloaded some
groceries from the car. "It's not locked."

"She doesn't lock her house?"

Nell appeared beside Paige. "No need. The protection
spells here are so strong, nothing will enter uninvited."

216

If only I'd known that before forking out for an expensive alarm system at the shop, thought Paige.

Paige followed Nell into the house. She had a feeling she'd follow Nell anywhere. While Calypso, Taran and Arley, especially Arley, shook her foundations, Nell made her feel safe. She had a calming quality about her that Paige clung to.

"Come and I'll show you around, Paige."

Ash Cottage was a pretty little stone structure tucked away at the edge of a forest near Tintagel in Cornwall. The cottage was a cozy little warren with stone walls and wood floors. While the decor looked like it hadn't changed for generations, there was no doubting that the house was a home. It had a wonderful light energy that sprang from centuries of laughter bouncing off the walls. Nell led Paige through a lounge room and dining room, a kitchen and a rather antiquated bathroom out the back. Then she took her up the higgledy-piggledy stairs to the two bedrooms.

"Are you and Arley together?" asked Nell.

Paige almost fell over. "Oh, no … nup, noooo. He's my mother's physiotherapist."

"That's a pity," Nell said simply. "But convenient for me. Do you mind sharing this room with me?"

Paige stuck her head around the doorway of the second bedroom and into a sunny little room with two single beds covered in patchwork quilts.

"Not at all. I'm happy to share." Secretly, Paige was relieved she'd be sticking close to Nell.

"Callie and Taran will be in the other bedroom, and Arley can have the lounge."

Paige put her bag on the bed near the window. She was tempted to crawl under the quilt then and there. She'd had a restless night's sleep, tossing and turning and regretting her plans to leave London with the others the following morning.

She'd spent the entire night trying to come up with a good enough reason to cancel.

"I'm not well. I think I've got food poisoning." And then she remembered that Nell had given her dinner, so she tossed and turned some more.

"I can't leave the shop." But that wasn't true. Sadie was thrilled to be there.

"I don't believe in fairies and think you're all as mad as my mother, and it frightens me." That was the truth, but Paige hated being rude or confrontational.

She turned to Nell, who was watching her from the door. "I'm not feeling myself."

Nell smiled kindly. "If you're half Fey but have only just found out, then you've spent your entire life not feeling yourself, Paige."

Paige put her hand on the windowsill to steady herself. "I don't believe fairies. I don't believe in ghosts. I don't believe in a big guy in the sky called God."

"Well, I know for a fact that two out of those three exist." Nell held out her hand. "And perhaps I'm just not seeing that God. Come on. Let's go downstairs."

*

Paige returned to a kitchen filled with laughter. Groceries were spread across the table, and Calypso was giving orders to both Taran and Arley.

"Put that in the fridge, Arley. And Taran, grab me a bottle of something to go with lunch."

Calypso looked up as Paige entered, and then added to Taran, "Take Paige down to the cellar with you."

Paige followed Taran down to the cellar, wondering what was so interesting that she needed to see it, and hoped it didn't involve chains.

Instead she entered an insulated room filled with bottles of homemade wine, herbs and magical brews.

"This is Calypso's brewery," said Taran with pride. "That corner is the mead ... over there she's brewing beer. Those racks of wine ... all hers. Elderberry, plum, apple and so on."

"It's impressive," Paige said. "What do the wines taste like?"

"The first night I was here, I expected to be poisoned," Taran laughed. "I remember teasing her about the first bottle tasting like camel's urine. But it was the best drop I'd had in ages."

He grabbed a couple of bottles and they headed back upstairs.

"I was just about to make some sandwiches. You hungry?" said Calypso.

Paige wasn't, but she didn't want a repeat performance of last night, so nodded.

Calypso's face beamed. She was clearly happy here. "Let's go digging for food."

She took off out the back door and the others followed. The back garden was an overgrown Eden of flowers, herb beds, veggie gardens and strange pots. There was a tilting wood paling fence on the boundary, with a gate that led directly into the forest behind.

"There's no path," said Paige.

"You're just not seeing it," Calypso said as she picked a tomato and some lettuce.

Arley gave a whoop. You've got goldthread here."

"There's silphion over there too."

"Oh, yeah, I see it."

Paige joined them to see what all the excitement was about. Arley pointed at a patch of dirt under a lemon tree.

"That, Paige, is something you won't see every day."

Paige stared at the dirt. "I don't see it now."

Arley looked at her and then back at the garden. "That little thistle-type vine with the yellow leaves?"

"Can't see it."

"Right there. Look closely."

"I can't see it, okay?" Paige snapped.

Nell appeared beside her. "She'll see it when she's ready."

"Ready for what?" Paige asked. "I have no idea what you're all talking about."

"I grow a lot of magical herbs here," Calypso explained. "I work by the threefold herbal law. If I find a plant that's endangered, I take some for my potions, and then replant the rest in three different spots. Because of their magical properties, not everyone can see them."

Paige looked around at the others in disbelief. "You can all see something there that I can't?"

Four heads nodded.

"I'm not sure if there's something wrong with me or with you." Paige looked at them with a mixture of defiance and fear. "Calypso, Nell, you've shared your background with me. As have you, Taran. You're all … witches." She stumbled slightly over the final word, but then gathered herself again and turned to Arley. "What's your excuse?"

"You mean, why can I see those plants?"

"Yes. Are you a witch too?"

"No." Arley chuckled, as though it was the most absurd thing he'd heard in ages. "I'm not a witch."

Paige's shoulders relaxed a little. Of course he wasn't.

Arley smiled at her. "I'm like you. I'm half Fey."

*

There was another knock on the door, but Paige ignored it. She had no intention of opening it until she'd worked out how she was going to make her escape. No car, no idea where she was going. Even her shoes weren't appropriate for long walks.

She heard whispered voices outside the door. Arley and Nell, by the sounds of it. And then they went silent and the door swung open and in walked Calypso.

Paige had a feeling that nothing ever stopped Calypso, let alone a flimsy closed door.

"What are you scared of, Paige?"

Wow, straight to the point.

"I'm not sure. All I know is that I feel unnerved by this whole place."

"And us."

Paige nodded. "I know it's rude, because you've been nothing but hospitable."

"But that might change at any moment and we might devour you or turn you into a toad, right?"

Paige took a step back. "Will you?"

"I haven't turned anyone into a toad since high school." Calypso laughed. "I'm joking, Paige. Those spells are so last century."

Now it was Paige's turn to laugh.

Calypso sat on the bed opposite Paige. "I am a witch, just like the sixteen generations of Shakespeare women before me. I'm proud of my family history. In all those hundreds of years of history, there was only one Shakespeare woman who deserved to be feared. And that's not because she was a witch. It's because she was a bitch."

"So she was a black witch and you're a white witch?"

"No such thing. Witches are witches. Just like any other faith, some will abuse it," Calypso said.

Paige stared at her and knew without a doubt that she was a good person. "So how are you connected to fairies?"

Calypso held her hands out open, as if laying herself bare. "As a witch, I'm closely connected to nature. That's why

I connect with nature spirits. In fact, I was initiated into the ancient healing and herbal arts in their realm when I was thirteen."

"Bloody hell, I was still playing with dolls at thirteen." Paige stared at her hands, neatly clasped on her lap. "What are fairies like?"

"What are humans like? All different, but with similar wants and needs." Calypso thought about it for a moment. "Fey folk work with nature, we work against it."

"If all this is true, what does being half-fairy make me? Or my daughter?"

"You'd be better off asking Arley that one."

Paige turned away. She blinked back tears. It was all too confusing. Here was this man she had turned to in her hour of need, and he believed himself to be the very thing she was struggling with.

"I know many people who are part Fey. No studies have been done on it, but from what I've observed, the human part of you is dominant. You can have kids. Once you are moved from their world, the Fey world, you age. You will die. You can go your entire life without knowing the Fey part of yourself." Calypso looked Paige square in the eye. "But I bet there have been signs."

"I didn't even like fairies when I was a kid," Paige snapped.

"That's probably a sign," Calypso said cheekily. "Have you ever seen things? Or known that things were going to happen before they did?"

Paige hated where this was headed. "Maybe. I don't know."

"Knock knock." Arley stuck his head into the room, as one would a tiger cage.

Calypso stood. "I'm going to finish making lunch."

She left, giving Arley a conspiratorial squeeze on the arm on her way out.

"You okay, Paige?" Arley looked genuinely concerned.

"I am. Nothing like being joke of the week."

"I'm not laughing at you."

Paige stood, face to face with Arley, challenging him. "You didn't find it funny, each time I came to your office, upset about my mother, talking about fairies?"

"No." He looked deep into her eyes. "I was too busy trying not to ..."

"Not to laugh?"

"Not to kiss you."

And with that he did. Arley drew Paige in, and kissed her, like no one had ever kissed her before. Long, deep, hot and filled with longing.

Paige slipped her arms around his neck and pressed her body to him, responding totally and utterly. For a moment, she forgot everything.

Finally, she pulled back. She searched his eyes. "Don't mess with me, Arley."

"I promise I'm not, Paige."

"This, you, fairies ... it's too much."

"No, it's exactly the right amount."

Paige laughed, surrendering to it all. "Arley, you're one of a kind."

"No ... there's you."

*

A few hours later, dressed in coats and boots, the group left Calypso's cottage and walked down a small lane and out onto the road. Paige had no idea where they were going, but for once that didn't matter. She was content just being there. It was a beautiful night. The stars were bright above them. The night air was icy but still. For a while there was no sound, apart from footsteps crunching on gravel, but eventually Taran broke the silence.

"Remember the first night you brought me down here, Cal?" Taran turned to the others to regale them with the story. "I was shit scared, and kept asking about werewolves. Calypso assured me there had been no sightings here for a while."

"Apart from that—" Nell stopped short when Calypso shot her a look.

Taran's face fell. "Are you saying there are werewolves here? I told you the English countryside was scary."

"Don't listen to him, Paige," Calypso shot over her shoulder. "He's a New York witch. Central Park is wild to him."

Arley stepped closer to Paige and slipped his hand through hers. "I think they're joking."

"I don't care anymore. Send down a UFO while you're at it. Bring on the zombie apocalypse. Might as well shatter every belief I've ever had."

Arley gave her a sexy smile. "Why not? It's a good time to start again.

Paige smiled and breathed deeply. She felt refreshed here. But that probably had more to do with Arley's kisses than the night air. How quickly things can shift. One minute she was frightened and wanting to go, and the next she was walking down to a magical grove at night with three witches and a man who thought he was half-fairy.

She needed to check the label on the wine she'd had at lunch.

They fell behind the others, happy to be in each other's company.

"I don't know anything about you, Arley."

"You know more than most people."

"You don't go around telling people you're half-fairy?" Paige teased.

"I'm not a fan of padded cells, so no." He gave her hand a squeeze. "I do understand how absurd it sounds."

"Do you have kids?"

"One of each. Quinn and Ren. Twins. Fifteen now, so trouble with a capital T."

Judging by the smile on Arley's face, Paige doubted they were trouble at all. "Do they live with their mother?"

"They float between us. It's amicable, we live a couple of streets apart, and the kids are fairly independent now, so come and go when they want." He drew her in closer. "I know you have a daughter, Linda. Jean adores her."

"Yes, they're close. We used to be, but our relationship has been strained since I divorced her father. Not sure why. He was hardly father of the year." Paige stopped walking and turned to Arley. "What does this mean for her? Are your kids quarter Fey?"

Arley looked thoughtful. "That's a tough one to answer. Quarter, half, percentages don't matter. My son identifies with being Fey. My daughter doesn't. But it's not even that simple. My daughter has gifts that she rejects for now, but in time I hope she accepts them." Arley placed his arm over Paige's shoulder and they once again followed the others. "How do you think Linda will react to all this?"

Paige gave a loud laugh. "Oh Arley, she'll have a shit fit."

They caught up to the others and walked deep into the woods.

"I can't see a thing. We should have brought a torch," said Paige.

"Won't need one soon," Calypso called over her shoulder.

They continued farther into the woods. Ferns and flowers rustled around their feet. Echoed whispers chimed through the darkness. And then Paige heard voices.

"She's back."

"She's here."

"Welcome, Calypso."

"Helloooo, Taran."

"Oooh, Nell."

"Arley." Like a sigh in the night.

Suddenly lights darted before them. Golden orbs floated around them, illuminating the way. Paige heard a symphony, the sound of flowing water, melodic as it descended. Eventually they stepped into Tintagel's natural glen, St. Nectan's waterfall.

"This is one of the most powerful sites in Great Britain," whispered Calypso. "It's a sacred well, and guarded by the Fey folk ... as you can see."

Paige would have had to be blind to miss the hundreds of orbs that lit the sky. Some floated; some perched on branches; some even came over for a closer look, allowing Paige a glimpse of the exquisite faces within the glowing orbs.

"Hello, Paige," one said.

"You know my name?"

"We know you." A thousand giggles tinkled through the air, making Paige feel that she'd just missed a joke.

The trees beside them rustled and parted and suddenly a handsome half-man, half-goat stood before them.

Just when Paige thought she was coping remarkably well with all the talk of fairies, and then the appearance of the talking orbs, this creature showed up and toppled her. She sat down and put her head between her knees, willing herself to not be sick.

"She is ill?" The faun looked annoyed by Paige's weakness.

"She's had a difficult few days, Adelein," Calypso said. "She's discovered she's half Fey."

"We know who she is. Daughter of Cadoc, stand before me."

Paige pulled herself together and did as she was told, clambering to her feet in front of this beast she'd only ever seen in children's books.

She looked at him. He was about her height but seemed so much taller. So much larger, stronger and alive in every way. She felt unworthy in his presence, until he lowered his head and bowed before her.

"Do *you* know who you are?" he asked, not unkindly.

"Not anymore. Perhaps I never did."

"You will learn."

Adelein glanced at the others. His eyes rested on Nell. "Your sister gave you my message?"

"Yes, she did. I don't know what *Cane Cata Juel* means, though."

"Because you're not ready yet."

Finally, he turned to Arley. "Cadoc thanks you."

Arley nodded and Adelein turned to leave.

"Wait," Paige said. "Will I meet my father?"

"He has been informed you are here." And the faun stepped behind the tree and vanished.

"Always fun meeting the faun," Taran whispered.

Calypso slapped him, giggling. "Shhh. Have some respect."

"He didn't even say hello to me." Taran pretended to be hugely offended.

Paige turned to Arley. "Why did he thank you?"

Arley cleared his throat a little. "I know your father."

Paige paled. "Please tell me we're not related."

Arley blanched. "Oh, Paige, I would never ... I just kissed you."

Paige looked relieved but she still stepped back when Arley tried to touch her.

Arley looked unapologetic. "I was asked to go to your mother. Cadoc knew she was planning to tell you about your background. I was sent to keep an eye on you."

"Sent from their world?"

"No, from London. Everything you know about me there is real. But I also visit my mother fairly regularly."

Paige felt dizzy. "*Fairy* regularly?"

"*Fairly* regularly," Arley said. "I was six when I was handed over to my human father. I remember my other home very clearly."

Paige took a deep breath. It was all too much to absorb. "Where the hell do I go from here, Arley?"

"Forward." He pulled her close again. "And I'll be with you every step of the way."

Paige looked around. "So where is my father?"

Calypso and Nell glanced at each other. "He's around."

"Doesn't he want to see me?"

"Paige," Arley said, "he sees you. But until you believe, how will you see him?"

*

Paige couldn't sleep. She crept out of the room, grabbing her warm clothes on the way, so as not to wake Nell. Downstairs, she dressed, pulled on her boots, and slipped out the back door. Then, using her flashlight, she began to walk. Her mind was awash with fairies and werewolves and magic. She felt as if there were two versions of herself, one sitting on each shoulder.

"What a ridiculous situation you've got yourself into, Paige. These people, their beliefs, why don't you just sign up for a cult while you're at it?" screeched one self.

"Don't listen, Paige. Trust your gut. You know in your heart that there is truth here." The other voice was convincing too.

"Truth here? Fairies? Magic? Are you nuts?"

"No, I'm not. And that's the point ... I'm practical. I'm intelligent. I'm no pushover. If this is happening to me, then there must be truth to it."

And on she walked, her breath coming out in clouds.

She thought about her childhood, something she rarely did. If she was honest, she had been a rather ... unusual child. But her mother had been strict. She'd been like a watchful hawk. Any glimmer of eccentricity in her daughter and she'd swoop.

Paige stopped. A strange language echoed through her mind, like a whisper from her past. She'd been so young, and she'd sit in their garden, singing and chatting to her invisible friends, in a language that would infuriate her mother. So much so that she'd moved them to an apartment with no garden.

And then there were the lights around her bed at night. Not unlike the orbs in the forest.

Wait a minute! The orbs. The faun. She'd seen them. *She'd seen them.*

Paige turned around and hurried back to Ash Cottage. She ducked around the side of the house to the back garden. She knelt down by the lemon tree and took her phone out of her pocket. Using the flashlight app, she pointed a thin beam of light at the ground.

Right there were two unusual plants, the likes of which she'd never seen before. One with yellow leaves, the other all the colors of the rainbow.

"How did I miss that?"

"You can't see what you don't believe," came a deep voice behind her.

Paige reeled back and shone the light up toward a man.

"Don't be afraid." He raised a hand to shield his eyes. "And perhaps you can turn that off. I have brought my own light."

Paige scrambled to her feet. It took her a moment to absorb the situation she was in. There were a number of orbs lighting the garden. In front of her stood a man who physically appeared younger than her, yet she knew he was her father.

She felt all of five years old in his presence.

His eyes shone. "I have been waiting for this moment."

Paige just stared at him, taking him in. He was tall, with black hair and almost translucent skin. His eyes were pale blue and sparkled like diamonds. He was beautiful, and left her feeling quite speechless. She knew that her reaction was probably a let-down, but she had no idea how to respond to him.

He tilted his head to one side, studying her. "Are you ill? You have a strange look on your face."

"That's just my face," Paige said. "And I'm shocked to meet you. It's a moment I always wished for, but now that it's here I have no idea what to do."

"We've met before. And I have always been here for you."

"Yes, thanks for the Christmas cards and child support," Paige snapped, but was then embarrassed she had.

He laughed. "You are just like your mother."

Paige was surprised. He meant that as a compliment. "Why was she scared of you?"

"She wasn't. She was scared of how she felt."

He smiled and Paige understood why her mother had fallen for him. He seemed to know what she was thinking.

"And I loved her. She is still my love," he said.

This surprised Paige. "I think you'll find there's a bit of an age gap now."

"Paige, child, human time does not exist where I am. How you see things is not my experience. I see things as they are here."

And with that Cadoc stepped toward her and kneeled, and Paige was about five again, standing in the garden of her childhood home. He embraced her, and she hugged him back.

"Mummy's moving us, Daddy."

"Don't worry, I will see you again."

"But what if I don't see you?"

"It doesn't mean I'm not here."

A voice called out from the house. "Paige, stop that babbling nonsense language. Everyone will think you're touched."

Her father gave her a wink. And suddenly, she was an adult again, standing eye to eye with him.

"Dawn is coming. I must go," he said.

"Will I see you again?"

"If you look properly."

Cadoc turned and walked toward the tilting back gate and Paige now saw the path beyond it that led into the forest. Orbs floated nearby. A warm light glowed beyond the trees. She could hear rustling, whispers and laughter. And at that moment Paige heard a familiar laugh above them all.

Her mother's laugh.

Jean appeared at the gate. She looked all of twenty, with loose hair and a flowing dress. She joined Cadoc, her face filled with happiness. Paige was frozen to the spot. Her mother blew her a kiss and then slipped her hand into Cadoc's before following him barefoot into the forest.

Paige blinked. The gate was closed again. The forest path gone. She noticed that there were lights on in Ash Cottage. She could hear voices. The sun was coming up, but surely it was still too early for the others to be awake.

"Paige?"

She turned. Arley was standing at the back door.

"Are you okay? Did they call you first?"

Paige shook her head. Her thoughts were jumbled. "What are you talking about?" She shivered, suddenly cold.

Arley was holding a blanket and wrapped it around her. "I just got a call from work. Paige, honey, I'm so sorry. It's Jean."

"Yes, I saw her." Paige's eyes sparkled.

"What do you mean, you saw her?"

"Here, with my father. I saw them."

Arley reached for her and held her tight. "Paige, your mother passed away last night."

Jean

Faeries, come take me out of this dull world,
For I would ride with you upon the wind …
William Butler Yeats

3.30 am, Christmas Eve

Jean woke in agony. She felt like she was being pressed under a rock. The pain shot down her arms and back. Christ, she needed Arley to do something about that. And then she smiled. He was with Paige.

It was enough to calm her for just a moment. But then it hit her chest.

She began to panic. She'd known for a while that her time was up. Her doctor had argued with her about telling Paige, but she couldn't. Paige would've acted like the dutiful daughter and remained by her side, and she'd exit this world knowing nothing had changed. It was only staring death in the eye that had made her re-evaluate everything. And that had been tough.

Jean knew she'd done what she'd thought was right, at the time. How could she ever foresee that by doing so, she'd color her daughter's world in grays and beige, when the world should be seen draped in rainbows. It was only then, when she finally admitted to herself what a dreadful mistake she'd made, that Arley had shown up.

Cadoc had sent Arley to her. And not only was he an excellent physiotherapist, he was exactly what Paige needed. It had taken her daughter a while to see it, but then seeing things clearly had never been Paige's strong point.

Jean's whole body lurched. She couldn't reach the buzzer. She tried to call out but her voice was locked in her throat. And just as fear was starting to truly grip her, she felt the shift.

A breeze entered the room. Lights danced around her bed. She could sense him near. The hands of the only man she'd ever loved lay softly on her. She opened her eyes, and he was there, leaning close, looking at her.

"You came for me."

"Did you ever doubt I would, my love?"

"No." She sat up. "Am I wearing lipstick?"

"You are. And you are beautiful."

Jean smiled. And with that, she slipped off the bed and into his embrace. And then together, they stepped into the mists.

The Book Club

If you want a happy ending, that depends, of course, on where you stop your story.
Orson Welles

Three weeks after Christmas

The women all sat in silence for a moment. They looked around at each other.

There had been tears, laughter, and moments of disbelief as each member of the book club told their story.

Paige was still quite fragile from losing her mother, yet her life was unfolding in ways she'd never thought possible. Eva was keeping an eye on her. The clutch of Eva's own grief had eased, so she was able to support her friend more now.

Clementine was curled up close to Michi. Both she and Debra were ecstatically happy at the moment, but that happiness was marred by Michi's announcement that she was moving back to Australia.

Amanda and Sadie both had a glow about them. Sadie was crazy about this guy she'd met, and couldn't wait for the others to get to know him. Amanda was taking things a little more slowly than Sadie, but then she was getting to know and love three people again.

And Tilda was barely recognizable to the others—although unlike most people, and certainly unlike Tilda herself, they had always seen her clearly. She was a valued and very much loved member of the group.

Paige grabbed a stack of books and handed them out. "I've taken the liberty of choosing the first book. Not long released, and I love the name."

Sadie took her copy and read out the title: "*The Happy Endings Book Club.*"

"How appropriate," Clementine said.

Michi turned her book over. "Who wrote it?"

"Jane Tara," Paige said.

"Never heard of her," Michi sipped her wine.

Tilda turned the book over and read from the back cover. "How do you see the world? Happy endings come not through events but through a shift in perception."

Sadie lifted her glass. "I'll drink to that."

"You'll drink to anything," laughed Amanda.

Clementine sat up, as though something had just occurred to her. "Do you realize, we all got our happy ending this Christmas?"

"Or beginning," Sadie said.

"Same thing," Tilda said.

"I'm just happy being here with you all now, in this moment." Eva looked across at Paige and smiled.

"So am I," said Paige.

"Let's toast this moment," said Amanda.

Everyone held their glasses high, and in unison said, "To this moment."

Paige nodded, feeling both the grief and utter joy of the past few weeks. She accepted them both for what they were, right now. It was all good. She looked around at her friends. "To happy endings."